What do you do when Mr. Right seems oh-so-wrong?

Holly Sinclair is ready to have it all. She's even found her Mr. Right—a steady, reliable guy who just needs a little convincing. Now all the former wild child has to do is free herself of her very inconvenient attraction to Jack Everett. Not only does the notorious playboy and tabloid king seduce her at her sister's wedding, he follows her to Paris! Suddenly, Holly is alone with Jack in the most romantic city in the world—and his family is leaping to the wrong conclusions...

The world's most infamous bachelor has finally met his match. If Jack was the type to settle down, Holly would be the woman of his dreams. There's just one hitch: Holly actually believes she wants to marry Mr. Oh-So-Boring. Intent on proving that she deserves someone better, Jack finds himself playing the role of the perfect boyfriend...a little too well. If he's not careful, he might just lose this game—and his heart.

THE ACCIDENTAL BOYFRIEND
A Chance Romance

Books by Maggie Dallen

The Chance Series
The Accidental Engagement
The Accidental Boyfriend
The Accidental Elopement

Published by Kensington Publishing Corporation

The Accidental Boyfriend

A Chance Romance

Maggie Dallen

LYRICAL PRESS
Kensington Publishing Corp.
www.kensingtonbooks.com

Lyrical Press books are published by
Kensington Publishing Corp. 119 West 40th Street New York, NY 10018

All Kensington titles, imprints, and distributed lines are available at special quantity discounts for bulk purchases for sales promotion, premiums, fund-raising, and educational or institutional use.

To the extent that the image or images on the cover of this book depict a person or persons, such person or persons are merely models, and are not intended to portray any character or characters featured in the book.

Special book excerpts or customized printings can also be created to fit specific needs. For details, write or phone the office of the Kensington Special Sales Manager:
Kensington Publishing Corp.
119 West 40th Street
New York, NY 10018
Attn. Special Sales Department. Phone: 1-800-221-2647.

Kensington and the K logo Reg. U.S. Pat. & TM Off.
Lyrical Press and the L logo are trademarks of Kensington Publishing Corp.

First Electronic Edition: May 2016
eISBN-13: 978-1-60183-467-6
eISBN-10: 1-60183-467-5

First Print Edition: May 2016
ISBN-13: 978-1-60183-468-3
ISBN-10: 1-60183-468-3

Printed in the United States of America

Chapter 1

Crayon drawings covered every inch of Holly's classroom walls. They needed to be taken down, but instead Holly sat cross-legged atop her desk, surveying the mess her second-graders had left behind.

Summer vacation technically started twenty minutes ago but she still had hours of cleanup and paperwork ahead of her before she was done for the school year. Picking up the stack of cards her students had given her as they filed out, Holly sifted through them with teary eyes. She stopped when she came to a hot pink card with a picture of Cinderella and Prince Charming on the cover.

One of her students had drawn an arrow to Cinderella and in big block letters wrote "Miss Holly" underneath. Holly's laugh sounded loud in the empty classroom. She had come to loathe the word "princess", thanks to the girls in her class with their rabid obsession for all things Disney, but *this*...this was adorable.

And so very fitting. Clapping a hand over her mouth, Holly smothered a near-hysterical giggle. It was true, for one night she had actually thought of herself as Cinderella.

Her breathing slowed as the memory of that night came back in vivid Technicolor. Her very own Prince Charming held her in his arms beneath the twinkling lights and twirled her in time with the music on the Italian veranda. The crowd was a blur to her because she only had eyes for one man, the man she'd had a crush on for years—Jack Everett.

"Do you need a hand in here?"

Holly came crashing back to the present as Donna, the grade school principal poked her head into her classroom.

"What? Oh, no. I got it, thanks." She scrambled off her desk and started to take down the giant panda bear poster that hung next to the chalkboard. It was the one poster she brought with her from school to school as she traveled and she'd hung it here earlier in the year when she'd taken over as a long-term substitute when old Mrs. Ferndale had been hospitalized with pneumonia.

"I'm glad I caught you," Donna said. She walked into the room and perched on the corner of one of the student's desks. A tall, heavyset woman, Donna dwarfed the small piece of furniture and made the warm, cozy classroom feel ten times smaller. "I heard from Mrs. Ferndale this morning and she's decided that she won't be coming back in the fall. She's opted to retire as I suspected she would."

Holly froze, her fingers clenching the poster so tightly that it ripped. Slowly she turned to face the other woman. She knew where this was going. This was what she had been hoping for since she moved back to her hometown of Oakdale, Ohio.

This was what she wanted. She should be excited. So why was there a cold pit in her stomach? Sliding into the chair behind the desk, she placed her hands on her knees to keep from fidgeting. She smiled at Donna with wide eyes, hoping she conveyed excited anticipation—although she had a funny feeling she just looked deranged if Donna's flinch was anything to go by.

"Oh really?" Holly said. Her voice came out slightly breathless.

Donna paused for a moment, seemingly weighing her words. "The students and their parents absolutely love you, Holly, and I know you've expressed interest in settling down here in Oakdale."

She paused, giving Holly room to respond. Holly just nodded; she didn't trust herself to speak. It was true. She'd decided to give up travel and adventure to return to her hometown in Ohio and have the life she wanted. Have the *family* she wanted.

"If you're interested," Donna said, a slow smile spreading across her face, "We would love to make your role here permanent."

Holly gasped as though surprised—as if this wasn't a possibility they'd been talking about at great length for the past few months. But now that it was here…she broke into a cold sweat but forced a smile to match the principal's. Of course she was nervous. Major life changes were scary. "Oh, Donna, thank you," she gushed.

Donna's smile grew as she waited for Holly to say the words that would make it official. Holly took a deep breath and opened her mouth to accept and instead she heard her voice say, "I need to think about it."

The words stunned Holly almost as much as they did Donna, who was blinking at her as though she couldn't comprehend the statement. After a moment though, she resumed her composure. "Of course, it's a big step. No one would expect you to make a hasty decision."

Holly latched onto that excuse. "Exactly. I'm not the type to act impulsively." *Liar.* "I'd really like talk it over with my family. And Benjamin, of course."

"Of course." Donna gave her a knowing look. "How are things with Benjamin?" She and Holly had become friendly since Holly joined the school and she was well aware of Holly's feeling for her longtime best friend. Donna was the only person she'd told who hadn't tried to talk her out of her quest to win back her high school sweetheart.

"Good," Holly said with a bit more enthusiasm than necessary. "Great, just great." Apparently the lies were pouring out of her mouth today.

"So he wasn't upset about the picture?"

Holly's smile froze in place. The picture. It had been more than a month since her sister's wedding, yet the local newspaper was still printing pictures of the big event. To be fair, a hometown girl marrying a billionaire in a lavish wedding in Tuscany was a tad more interesting to readers than the library's latest fundraiser. But still. Let it go already, people.

Unfortunately, one of the pictures that her mother had kindly sent to the newspaper featured Holly dancing with Jack, the world-famous tech genius. They were gazing at each other in a way that may have led some viewers to the wrong conclusion. Like that they were in love or something. Which couldn't be further from the truth. She was pretty sure Jack hated her after the way that night ended—if he hadn't already forgotten about her.

She had been making such progress with Benjamin when that stupid picture was printed. "No," she said, trying not to sound as bummed as she felt. "He wasn't upset at all."

Sadly that was the truth. She hadn't expected him to be angry—it's not like they were dating—but she had hoped he'd be a tad bit jealous. Or a whole lot jealous.

Before she'd left for the wedding, she'd made it clear that she wanted to take their relationship to the next level but Benjamin was worried that dating would ruin their friendship. And he still wasn't convinced that settling down in Oakdale was what Holly really wanted. As if moving back home and taking a teaching job at her old school wasn't evidence enough that she was serious about changing her ways.

That picture popping up in the paper certainly hadn't helped her cause.

Donna was giving her an annoyingly sympathetic look so Holly amped up the smile. "Besides, Paula Dunhop's annual Oakdale Charity Ball is coming up this weekend so I imagine my silly picture will no longer be making the news."

Donna's eyes widened in surprise and then she cringed. "Actually . . . that's not the picture I was referring to."

Holly's whole body stiffened. "What? What other picture is there?"

Donna was already digging through her gigantic purse. She brandished an issue of *People* magazine with a flourish and handed it to Holly. "Page thirteen."

As Holly flipped to the page, her stomach plummeted. What if someone had someone caught their—

"That certainly looks like a kiss to me," Donna said.

Holly couldn't look up at her co-worker, she was hypnotized by the image in front of her. Jack's tuxedo jacket was draped around her shoulders and she was tucked against his side. He was leaning in and she was gazing up. They weren't actually kissing but it was clear what was about to happen seconds after the shot was captured.

Holly's mind was racing and, if she was being honest with herself, so was her pulse. Jack looked good. No, he looked amazing. Just looking at the picture, she was transported back to that moment—that magical, fairytale evening, which was rapidly becoming a nightmare that would not end.

She'd been trying to forget that night for an entire month. Thirty days of trying not to think about Jack, or that kiss...or what happened after that kiss. It was like not thinking of a pink elephant once someone has told you not to. Impossible. But maybe, just maybe, she would be able to forget the playboy hottie if everyone would stop constantly reminding her of that night!

But nooooo. First her hometown paper and now this. She slammed the offensive magazine closed and took a deep breath. What had they been talking about? Oh yes, Benjamin.

Oh no, Benjamin.

Her chest tightened and she forced herself to take a deep breath. What were the odds that he had seen the magazine? Slim to none. If there was ever a man who did not follow pop culture gossip, it was Benjamin. Although...he did have two sisters who loved gossip more than life itself. And he lived in a town that was obsessed with all things Jack Everett and the Sinclair sisters. Oh crap, if he hadn't seen it already it was just a matter of time before he did.

Her chair made a loud creaking noise as she pushed it back and hopped out of her seat. She grabbed a box that was half packed and started heading toward the door. "Donna, I should go. I've got to see Benjamin but, uh, I'll get back to you about the teaching job, okay?"

She was out the door before Donna had a chance to respond.

* * * *

Holly found Benjamin quickly. Of course she did. That was the beauty of Benjamin—he was predictable.

She met him in his driveway seconds after he pulled in. "Hey, what are you doing here?" he asked, unloading his briefcase from the passenger side of his car. "I thought I was picking you up tonight so we could celebrate the last day of school."

She should tell him about the offer for a permanent job but she couldn't seem to get the words out of her mouth. Instead, she tucked a stray curl behind her ear and sauntered over to him with a grin. "Aren't you happy to see me?" she teased. She'd meant it to sound coy, maybe trigger a bit of flirtatious banter, but he ignored the tone and answered the question.

"Of course I'm happy to see you, I'm just surprised is all. I thought we'd agreed on a plan for tonight."

She resisted the urge to sigh. After all, his ability to make plans and stick to them was what she liked about him. She followed him up the walkway to his front door and into the lovely comfort of his house.

He dropped his briefcase near the front door and led the way toward the kitchen. "So did Donna have any news on Mrs. Ferndale?"

"Um …" Before she could reply, Holly noticed the packed luggage sitting in the hallway. "Going somewhere?"

Benjamin never went anywhere. Ever. He was born in Oakdale and had lived there his whole life. His idea of an exotic vacation was to drive one hour north to a state park and go camping.

"Yeah, the company is sending me to Paris for a conference. I leave in the morning."

Holly's mouth fell open and it took her a moment to form words. "Paris? Really? That's awesome."

He shrugged, "It's just a work trip."

And then it struck her, "When were you going to tell me?"

"Tonight at dinner." He glanced over to where she stood frozen in place by the doorway. "What's wrong?"

Her hands clenched at her sides. Unbelievable. Benjamin—*her* Benjamin—was finally taking a trip, and to *Paris*, of all places, and he hadn't thought to tell her, let alone invite her along.

He was watching her, his brows drawn together in concern. "Are you okay?"

"Yes," she said, a little too quickly. She cleared her throat and tried again. "So why is your work sending you on this trip?"

Benjamin worked in IT and approximately three sentences into his story about the conference, her eyes glazed over. 'Just a work trip,' he'd said. Just a work trip...*to the most romantic city in the world.*

Holly had laid all the ground work. She'd dropped hints, flirted and instigated deep, meaningful talks about the possibility of a future together. For the love of God, she had done everything short of pounce on this man and beg him to marry her. And he couldn't even be bothered to make one romantic gesture. Did she have to do everything around here?

"Holly?" He was eyeing her warily, like she might spontaneously combust.

She forced her hands to unclench and took a deep breath. She had to get out of there before she lost it. She had spent the past few months trying to prove to Benjamin that she had matured since they'd last dated, way back in high school, and that she was now emotionally stable and even-keeled.

Picking her purse back up from the table where she'd just set it down, she feigned a calm she did not feel. "I think we should take a rain check on dinner. You're going to need your sleep before the big trip and I've had a long day." She faked a loud yawn as she reached for the door. She would walk out of there without causing a scene if it killed her.

* * * *

Later that night Holly was camped out on the couch in her apartment. After living out of suitcases for so many years, she'd learned to get by with the necessities, which meant that all of her earthly belongings barely filled the spacious loft's closet. Her parents had given her their old couch and she'd invested in a good bed. Other than that, her place was depressingly spare.

It was more depressing than ever tonight, with Chinese food cartons scattered around the couch and an empty bottle of wine beside her. What was she doing with her life? That was the theme of this particular pity party. Had she made the wrong decision coming back here to this town? To Benjamin?

Maybe. But what was the alternative? To go back to the life she had been living, a life filled with adventure and travel and new experiences . . . and men just as flaky and afraid of commitment as she was. While men like that led to a fun time—okay, a *really* fun time—she wanted more from a relationship than one night stands or casual flings. She was ready for a commitment.

She and Benjamin didn't have the kind of mad, passionate love that her sister had found with her new husband but so what? Passion wasn't everything. Holly and Benjamin had history and, more importantly, trust. Weren't her parents always telling her that was the foundation for a solid marriage? She and Benjamin could be happy together. She just had to make him see it.

If he wouldn't woo her, she would have to do it herself. Adrenaline erased the lazy malaise she'd been wallowing in all evening. She sat up straight and threw off the quilt she'd been huddled under. She'd never been one to sit by and let an opportunity pass her by, why would she start now? Flipping open her laptop, she started to assemble a plan.

Her fingers flew over the keyboard as she sorted through flights with a well-practiced eye. Her heart was racing with excitement. She would be alone with Benjamin in the most romantic place in the world.

Her traitorous mind flashed on a certain villa in Tuscany. One of the most romantic places in the world, she mentally amended.

She took a deep breath and hit "Buy ticket."

Paris, here I come.

* * * *

Sixteen hours and multiple cups of coffee later, Holly arrived.

She'd gotten some sleep on the plane but she was still exhausted, jet lagged and feeling the after effects of that bottle of wine she'd downed the night before.

She exited the train station near the Montmartre neighborhood, where she'd stayed the last time she was in Paris between teaching gigs in Prague and Istanbul. All symptoms of a hangover disappeared in a rush of excitement.

The sights and sounds of Paris were invigorating—a noisy bustle of people and cars filled her senses, and the smell—oh, the smell. Holly inhaled deeply. She had learned that every city had a unique scent and Paris's *parfum* was intoxicating, a heady mix of fresh baked bread and exhaust fumes.

Holly had no trouble finding a room at a hostel. As soon as she was settled, she found a landline in the hostel's common room and pulled out a pre-paid phone card. Ivy could spread the word to their parents; she'd always been the best buffer when breaking news to their parents. Like, for example, that she'd run off to Paris on a whim to find her future husband.

"I need you to tell Mom and Dad something," she started the conversation.

Ivy groaned. "Oh no. What did you do?"

Holly ignored that. "First, how are you feeling?"

"Like a whale," Ivy said. "A beached whale."

"Well, if you've gotta be beached, you could do worse than a villa in Tuscany," Holly said. Ivy's husband was newly reunited with his family in Italy and the couple opted to stay there after the wedding to give Daniel a chance to reconnect with his relatives.

"True," Ivy said with a laugh. "I've got a small army waiting on me, and they're all being led by the General." "The General" was Ivy's affectionate nickname for Daniel.

"Is he driving you crazy yet?" Holly teased.

She could practically hear Ivy's eyes roll. "The man is insane. He won't let me do anything for fear I'm going to tire myself out. Holly, I swear to God…he tried to spoon feed me my cereal this morning."

Holly burst out laughing at the image. "That's kinda sweet in a weird way."

"It really is," Ivy said with a sigh that was so sappy and swooning, it was Holly's turn to roll her eyes.

"So what's up?" Ivy asked.

"Benjamin went to Paris for a conference," she started.

"Yeah, I know, Mom told me."

"Mom told you?" Incredible. Her mother had known he was going to Paris but he hadn't thought to tell her.

"Yeah, his mom told our mom and you know Mom calls every day to check in on the baby. I get all the juicy Oakdale gossip."

Holly took a deep breath and shut her eyes. "I followed him," she said on a rush of air.

"Wait, what? You followed who?" Ivy asked.

"Benjamin. I followed him to his conference."

There was a moment of silence before Ivy said, "But, why?" The sound of complete and utter incomprehension was as comforting as it was annoying. Ivy had always been the good one—she would never, ever go running after a boy.

"Because it's romantic," Holly explained.

"Oh my God, you have got to be kidding me. Are you still on this kick? You can't honestly believe that you and Benjamin are destined to be together, I thought you were moving on. I mean, when I saw you and Jack at the wedding, I thought—"

"Nothing happened between me and Jack!" The phrase came out louder than anticipated and Holly rubbed a hand over her face.

The echoing silence was as obvious as if Ivy outright said the words, "Yeah, right."

Maybe she was protesting a bit too much but every time Jack's name was mentioned—and it seemed like it was mentioned daily in her family—it was almost always followed by some comment about how great they looked together or what a wonderful couple they'd make. Jack was exactly the type of guy she'd have gone for in the past but now that she'd turned over a new leaf? Never gonna happen.

Benjamin on the other hand....

"We would make the perfect couple," Holly said.

"You and Jack?" Ivy asked. She honestly sounded confused.

Holly gripped the phone tighter. Why was everyone so obsessed with that man? "No, keep up. Me and Benjamin."

Ivy's sigh was borderline condescending. "You *were* the perfect couple—*in eighth grade.* Times have changed. You've changed. There's a whole big world out there filled with—"

Holly raised a hand to interrupt her sister as though Ivy was in the hostel room and not lounging on a veranda in Tuscany with half of Italy waiting on her hand and foot. "I've been out in the world, Ivy. I'm not some kid who's never left Oakdale, okay? I'm older than you."

"By one year," Ivy said, most likely out of habit more than anything else. When she spoke again, her voice was softer. "What's this really about, *Holiday*?"

There it was. Her old nickname, the one that made her feel like a seven-year-old with skinned knees and a deep desire to live in a treehouse. She considered telling her sister about what had happened the year before, the reason she'd returned to Oakdale. But then she pictured Ivy with her big belly and her doting husband and shut her mouth—there was no way she could understand. Ivy might be able to sympathize but she could never understand.

"Listen, I've got to get going. Just tell Mom and Dad that I'm in France and I'll check in every few days so I don't miss the big announcement, 'kay? Tell them that I'll meet up with you all in Italy—"

She heard Ivy start to protest, "Wait, France? But, Holly, Benjamin—"

Holly hung up with a grin. She'd known her sister would argue, it's what sisters do—especially *her* sister.

Chapter 2

Jack was fairly certain he was hallucinating when Brunelli placed the open magazine in front of him and Daniel. After a month of seeing Holly constantly in his mind's eye, he was sure he'd conjured her up.

Daniel cursed under his breath in a way that suggested Jack should fear for his life. No, he definitely hadn't made this up. He and Holly were featured prominently in the center spread, she looking ethereal with her blond curls and pale blue gown, and him looking...well, *smitten*, was the only word to describe it. He leaned in to take a closer look. Good God, it almost looked like he was—

"You're in love," Brunelli declared, smacking the magazine with the back of his hand as though his words were a decree from above. The third partner in EverTech, the old Italian was the biggest romantic Jack had ever met.

"What? I am not in love," Jack protested.

Daniel did not look amused. "How did this happen?"

"What do you mean, 'how did this happen'? We were having fun." Jack gestured toward the veranda as though the photographer was still out there. "How was I supposed to know there was somebody taking our picture?"

Daniel, who had been more and more on edge as his wife's pregnancy progressed, looked just about ready to throttle Jack.

"Wait a second," Jack said, feeling a tad defensive in the face of Daniel's wrath. "Who am I dealing with here, overbearing business partner or overprotective brother-in-law?"

Daniel opened his mouth to answer but stopped as though stumped. Jack looked from Daniel to Brunelli, who just shrugged.

"I did nothing wrong here," Jack said, pointing to the picture.

"Are you sure? Because it looks like you're about to," Daniel said. At that Brunelli nodded his agreement. Jack looked back at the picture. It did look incriminating. But for once, he could tell the truth, even though the truth sucked.

"I'm positive," Jack said, giving them his best look of innocence. "I wouldn't lie to you guys. We shared one innocent kiss"—okay, that was a stretch, it was passionate as hell and about as innocent as the devil—"but that's where it ended." He pointed to the beautiful blonde with blue eyes and the face of an angel. "We had a fun night together but even I wouldn't try to seduce an innocent. She's a second grade teacher from Ohio, for God's sake, give me some credit."

That much was true and Daniel knew it. The type of women Jack got involved with were worldly and experienced—the type who knew what they were getting into and had no delusions of happily ever afters. Jack didn't do commitments; he wasn't built that way. People who counted on him had a tendency to get hurt and he'd figured out long ago that it was best to keep his distance. The press may have declared him a heartbreaker but he had no intention of actually breaking hearts.

Daniel looked unconvinced. "If you mess with Ivy's sister and she gets hurt, there will be hell to—"

"Daniel!" Ivy's voice called out from the hallway.

All three men scrambled to hide the magazine as Ivy approached. Jack wasn't the only one terrified of her reaction—the baby was due in a matter of weeks and her emotional stability was in something of a free fall.

She came waddling in with Brunelli's eldest granddaughter, Lucia, following closely behind her. Lucia was shaking her head and giving Daniel a wide-eyed look of warning.

Jack exchanged looks with the other two men. Oh no, she'd seen the picture.

When Ivy came to a stop before them, out of breath from the long walk inside, Jack was ready to confess.

"I swear, Ivy, I didn't know—"

"Daniel, we have to go to Paris," Ivy said at the same time.

Jack stopped midsentence and turned to Daniel, whose jaw had dropped open in surprise. Daniel got to his feet and gently ushered her into a chair at the table. "Sweetheart, what are you so worked up about?"

"I need to get to Paris," she said as Daniel propped up her feet and poured her a glass of lemonade. Watching Daniel, the coldhearted, ruthless tycoon, become a doting nursemaid over the past few weeks had been a constant source of amusement for Jack and Brunelli.

"Honey, you know you can't fly in your condition," Daniel said.

"Then you need to go to Paris," she told him.

Daniel sat back in his chair and, in a calm voice of reason, said, "I was rather hoping to be present at the birth of my first child."

Ivy let out a sigh but she nodded her agreement.

"What's wrong?" he asked. "Maybe we can come up with a solution that doesn't involve either of us flying to Paris today."

"It's Holly," Ivy started.

Brunelli's eyes shot to Jack, who subtly shifted in his seat so he could run away, if necessary. No one in this room knew his tendency to love 'em and leave 'em as well as Ivy did and if she thought for one second that her sweet, innocent sister was another notch on his bedpost, well she'd be a very pregnant, but very frightening, force to be reckoned with.

"What about Holly?" Brunelli asked, his gaze still locked on Jack.

Ivy blew an errant auburn curl out of her face. "She's on a wild goose chase in Paris."

"Holly's in Paris?" Daniel said.

"Paris, *France*," Ivy clarified, as though there was some doubt as to where Paris was located.

"I thought Holly was coming back to Italy to meet the baby next month," Jack said. Not that he'd given it much thought or anything. He'd just rehearsed what he would say to her about six thousand times. Every time, it started with an apology. He was still ashamed of the way he'd ended things that night.

"She's still coming here, but she decided to go to Paris first so she could chase after some guy."

Jack's brain went black. Before he could come up with a nonchalant way of asking why the hell Holly would be chasing after anyone—the woman was a goddess—Ivy was off on a tangent.

"This is just like her. Act first, think later. No, more like act first, think never. And now I have to tell my mom and dad that Holly ran away. I mean, she's a grown woman, sure, but they still worry and it's not like—"

Daniel put a hand over hers and it seemed to bring Ivy back to the present. She got a dreamy look on her face as she gazed adoringly at her new husband for a moment. Then she was right back to her old self.

"I'm worried about her," she said. Her lips pressed together in a thin line as she crossed her arms over her chest.

Jack couldn't take it anymore. "Who's the guy?"

All eyes turned to him and he cleared his throat a bit. Perhaps that had come out a tad more…*intense* than he'd intended.

He tried again. "I mean, why is she chasing after this guy?" Leaning back in his chair he tried to project calm indifference but he didn't miss the odd looks he got from the others at the table.

"Benjamin," Ivy said his name on an exasperated sigh.

"Who's Benjamin?" Now it was Daniel's turn to sound a touch too angry, but it didn't seem to strike anyone as odd coming from the overprotective brother-in-law.

"Is she in trouble?" Brunelli asked. The old man's wrinkled brow was creased more than usual in concern.

"No, not really," Ivy said.

Jack let out a pent up breath.

"She just wants to marry him."

Jack froze. "What?" Luckily his not-so-manly screech was drowned out by similar outburst from everyone at the table. "So are you telling us that Holly has a *boyfriend*?" His voice sounded strange to his own ears. Oh God, he sounded like a jealous lover.

Daniel and Brunelli both turned to him with a glare and Brunelli gave a short nod toward the magazine, which was currently jutting out from beneath Jack's behind.

Lucia answered this one, a hint of a smile hovering on her lips. "*Had* a boyfriend. He's the one that got away." She reached over to grab a grape from the fruit bowl in the middle of the table. "I think it's romantic that she's going after him."

Ivy rolled her eyes. "Benjamin is sweet and all, but...."

But? Jack waited for her to continue but she just shook her head and sighed. *But what?* Was he a bad influence on her? Was he a player? Would he break her heart?

"It doesn't matter why she followed him, the problem is, Holly followed him to the wrong Paris."

Daniel frowned at her in concern. "Have you gotten too much sun today, sweetheart?" He reached over to place a hand on her forehead to check for a fever but she swatted him away.

"Holly is in Paris, *France*," she stressed again, "and Benjamin is in Paris, *Texas*."

There was a quiet beat as everyone digested the fact that Texas had a Paris of its own.

Lucia's eyes widened in horror. "So Holly is alone in France and Benjamin is—"

"At an IT convention in the lone star state," Ivy finished. "Yeah, that sums it up."

"Can't we call her?" Daniel asked.

Ivy shook her head. "Her phone is off since she's out of country. She won't check in again for days, maybe a week. And she's terrible at checking email."

"Do you know where she's staying?" Brunelli asked.

"No, she didn't say. But calling would do no good. She always uses different names when she travels."

Jack and the others looked at one another in confusion and Ivy added, "You know, like celebrities use?" At their silence she mumbled, "You guys don't know Holly very well, do you?"

Jack opened his mouth to protest but stopped himself. Of course he didn't know her well, they'd only spent one night together. One incredible night—but still.

Daniel reached over to grab his wife's hand. "Don't worry, honey, I'll go to Paris and make sure your sister is safe." Ivy gave him a grateful smile.

Jack's heart was pounding faster than usual and he was suddenly sweltering despite the air conditioning. Holly was close. Well, closer than the States, at least. She was on the continent, just a short plane ride away. The words were out of his mouth before he could think it through. "No, I'll go."

* * * *

Everyone turned to Jack in surprise and he shifted uncomfortably under their stares. "What? We all know Ivy could go into labor at any moment and nobody wants her or Danny stressing out about him not making it back in time."

Ivy and Daniel shared a look that said he was right.

"Are you sure?" Ivy asked.

"Of course. I've been meaning to take a trip to Paris to visit my brother and his wife." That was an outright lie but it sounded good and made his sudden eagerness to head to France slightly less bizarre.

So he was excited to see her. He could admit it to himself. He liked her. There. He admitted it. They didn't have a future together, obviously, and there was a good possibility that she hated him right now but still, he liked her. He wanted them to be friends.

They would be in one another's lives forever thanks to Ivy and Daniel and the new little baby on the way. He might as well get this apology over with and start making amends.

Ivy seemed happy with this new solution but Daniel was eyeing him. Jack could practically see the gears turning. When Ivy and Lucia left, happy in the knowledge that Holly would be found and not be left wandering the streets of Paris, France, for eternity, he was left alone once again with Daniel and Brunelli.

"What's this all about?" Brunelli asked.

"Don't tell me you suddenly developed an urge to eat croissants," Daniel said.

"I told you, my brother moved there with his wife and—"

"Since when are you and your brother on speaking terms?" Daniel asked.

Jack grabbed some fruit and ignored the comment, focusing instead on juggling the apples and orange he held in his hands. "What's your solution?" he asked. "You don't want to leave Ivy. Are you really going to ask Grandpa here to go on this wild goose chase? No offense, Brunelli."

The old man shrugged off his apology, "It's true, I'm old."

Daniel was still watching him with narrowed eyes. "Does your sudden desire to go to France have anything to do with this?" He pulled the magazine out from underneath Jack and held it up accusingly.

"I told you, nothing happened." Jack snatched the magazine out of his hand. "Nothing of significance, anyway." Unless you found amazingly perfect moments significant. In which case, maybe he'd lied.

"Look, I don't know how she feels about me right now or about the picture, but I do know that I owe her an apology—" He held up a hand to stop the question that was coming. "I want to make things right. For Ivy's sake and for Holly's. I don't want things to be weird between us."

Daniel leaned back in his chair, apparently accepting Jack's explanation.

Ivy came back into the room and handed Jack a sheet of paper. "I don't know if this will help but here are the names of some hostels where she might be staying. I know she likes this neighborhood."

"Hostels?" Brunelli spit out the word with distaste. "Holly can't stay at a place like that, I refuse to allow it. Jack, you will bring her to my pied-a-terre. No friend of mine will stay with…backpackers." The word backpackers sounded like a curse word coming from Brunelli.

"Sure thing, boss," Jack said, as Brunelli continued to grumble about filthy backpackers. He looked over the list of hostels. They were all in Montmartre, a well-known tourist destination.

"So Holly has been to Paris before," Jack said, taking the paper from her. "That's good." Ivy gave him a funny look and he added, "At least she won't be intimidated by the big city."

That made Ivy laugh. "Trust me, Jack, there's not much in this world that intimidates Holly."

* * * *

Maybe it was time to phone a friend.

Holly was slumped over in her stool at the bar in the lobby of a hotel. The fifth hotel she'd been to that day, to be exact. Jet lagged and exhausted from trekking all over the city, she was ready to call it quits.

Maybe tomorrow she'd call her mom and ask her to find out where Benjamin and his IT buddies were hiding out. The thought of explaining herself to her mother was not at all appealing. Maybe she would call around to some other hotels tonight. Her sluggish brain refused to even contemplate next steps without a glass of wine in her hand.

Flagging down the bartender at the other end of the bar, she opted for choice number three—declare temporary defeat and enjoy the best city in the world while she could. After all, once she and Benjamin started a family she couldn't traipse off across the world on a whim anymore.

Pushing aside a sudden tightness in her chest, Holly reminded herself that having a family would be worth the sacrifice.

She longed for a husband and a family and the white picket fence. She just hadn't realized it until a year ago—until the miscarriage. It took having a family and losing it to make her see what was important in life.

The father had been another casual fling—one in a long line of infatuations and exciting, passionate romances that ultimately led nowhere. Before she could say "baby" he was out the door and out of her life with no more than a "ciao, babe."

The miscarriage had hit her hard. Harder than she would have expected. She'd freaked when the strip turned blue but there had been excitement there alongside fear. She hadn't realized how attached she'd gotten until it was gone.

She'd cried for weeks.

And then she'd booked a flight home. Back to her family, her hometown, and her first love—Benjamin. He was the obvious choice. If she was going to settle down, why not be with her best friend—a man who was stable and reliable and responsible and…basically, everything she was not. He would make an amazing father someday. The now-familiar mental image of Benjamin standing at her side as they gazed in adoration at their little bundle of joy was enough to make her heart squeeze painfully.

Yes, it would all be worth it once she had her family.

The waiter poured her a glass of red and she swirled it for a moment before raising it in salute. "Goodbye adventures, I'll miss you most of all."

Surrounded by happy couples and loudly chatting friends, Holly scrounged in her bag for something to read. She was sure her e-reader was hiding somewhere in the depths of her oversized purse—her Mary

Poppins bag, as Benjamin liked to call it. Her fingers curled around a magazine and she pulled it out with a sigh.

It was that damn magazine with her stupid picture in it. She'd picked up a copy at the airport, despite her best intentions to ignore it on the stands. She couldn't help taking one more look. And then another once she was on the plane. And now it was there in her hands and she found her traitorous fingers flipping it open to page thirteen.

It wasn't because she wanted another glimpse of Jack, she told herself. Of course not. She just wanted to see it one more time with an objective eye; maybe it would help her figure out what to say to Benjamin once he saw it. Holly sighed; she had resigned herself to the fact that it was only a matter of time before he did.

If she found him quickly enough she planned on being the one to tell him so she could make sure he didn't read anything into it.

Her heart skipped a beat as the pages fell open to the incriminating photo. She took a sip of wine to wet her suddenly dry mouth and forced herself to study the picture—she had to get over this ridiculous infatuation. And that's what it was. It was just a harmless crush. Or at least it *had* been harmless when he was just tabloid eye candy and she was just another tabloid junkie.

But then he'd gone and become a real person. He'd come crashing into her sister's life and then hers. She took another, larger gulp of wine as she studied the picture. She couldn't believe this was happening *again*.

Few people knew the real story of how Jack came to know the Sinclair sisters and that's the way they had to keep it. If anyone discovered the truth…well, no one looked good in the harsh light of the truth.

It had all started with an incriminating photo of Jack and Ivy that made it look like Jack was proposing. Taken totally out of context, of course, as the two had practically been strangers at the time. The photo became a tabloid sensation and everyone got the wrong impression.

Ivy was coerced into playing the part of Jack's fiancée in order to save a business deal with Brunelli but when Ivy fell in love with Jack's best friend, Daniel, the fake engagement came to an abrupt end, and Jack was cast as the rejected, heartbroken lover.

Until now.

There beneath the photo on page thirteen, the caption read: "Jack Everett shows he's the bigger man by coming out to support the union of his ex-fiancée and his business partner at their wedding in Italy last month. Perhaps his ability to forgive and forget is thanks to the beautiful blonde who sources say never left his side."

Holly drained the rest of her glass.

The wine was delicious and went directly to her head, enveloping her in a lovely warmth from her head down to her toes and taking the harsh edge off of her jangled nerves. She slipped the magazine back into her purse. That was a problem for another day. For tonight, she was going to enjoy herself.

She was in no rush to get back to her hostel, where she was sharing a room with three loud, college-age Polish girls who didn't speak a word of English. One glass of wine led to two and then a lovely elderly gentleman offered to buy her a round and really, who was she to refuse a sweet old man?

It was in a state of giddy, lovely tipsiness that she sauntered back into her hostel. The ground floor had a bar area that was popular with expats—a sort of backpackers' United Nations. She'd spent a lot of time at that bar the last time she'd stayed. Her boyfriend-of-the-hour, Lyon, had worked at a nightclub nearby and he'd meet her there for drinks before, during, and after his shift. Holly hesitated for a moment. But no, that was years ago, there was no way Lyon still haunted this bar.

She headed toward the bar area. Had it always smelled so strongly of smoke? Probably. Ooh, but that pool table was new. A group of young men were standing around it. Almost all looked to be too young for her. They had the straight-out-of-college look going on with their backward-facing baseball caps and faded T-shirts. For a brief moment, Holly had a stab of longing to be back in her early twenties; footloose and carefree. Back then she would take off to a new destination on a whim, never worrying about those pesky grownup things like health insurance or pension plans or declining fertility rates.

Granted, this trip to Paris had been a whim. But that was different. She was on a mission.

She sauntered over to the pack of English speaking young'uns and caught enough of the conversation to know that they were betting on the next game. One of the boys closest to her threw out a number that made her jaw drop.

No college grad had that kind of money unless they were tapping into a trust fund. Unless… She wandered closer to the group to get a better look. Yup. They were techies, the early twentysomethings who could be found in droves in Silicon Valley and who tended to travel together in packs. The famous website logos on their faded T-shirts were far better marketing than business cards. Whoever the poor sucker they were gambling against, he was in over his head.

The poor sucker was currently out of eyesight but a shockingly familiar voice said, "Bring it on, boys. Double or nothing."

Holly's saunter turned into a stumble. It sounded like—but no, it couldn't be. But it really sounded exactly like—

A cheer went up from the group of boys and several of the boys started chanting their new hero's name. "Jack, Jack, Jack...."

A wave of dizziness struck her as she froze in the middle of the room. *Oh. My. God.*

Before she could wrap her head around the fact that Jack Everett was here—*here* at her hole in the wall hostel, home to vagabonds, students, and the dreaded backpackers—the crowd before her parted and there he was, framed between a programmer from Twitter and a digital marketing consultant from Facebook. Or at least, that's what she assumed they did.

But they didn't matter. The boys fell away along with the rest of the world at the sight before her. All she could see was the handsome man with a five o'clock shadow and a devilish grin. His navy button-down was wrinkled and his jeans and shoes were faded and worn. He didn't look like the genius tech tycoon who'd created the trendiest devices of the day.

The last time she'd seen him he was wearing a tux, the very picture of glamour and wealth, but today he looked like an average Joe, someone you'd sit next to at a sports bar or stand in line with at the bank. Except not. He was the guy who would play that guy in a movie. Because he was that guy times a million. He was the living, breathing definition of sexy and handsome and...oh dear God, he was playing with a pool stick.

Her heart beat so quickly it threatened to leap out of her chest. That was it—he was young Tom Cruise in *The Color of Money*. Not fair, not fair! Young Tom Cruise was her biggest weakness. How did he know that?

Get it together, Sinclair. She took a deep, steadying breath as the synapses in her brain struggled to make sense out of what she was seeing. What was he doing here? This could not be real. How much wine had she ingested? She really should have had dinner. It was a dream, it was just a dream. He bent over to take a shot and...oh Lord, that butt was definitely *not* a dream.

Her mouth opened of its own accord. "What are you doing here?"

If a record had been playing, it would have scratched to a halt. All the joking and laughter came to an abrupt halt at the sound of her high-pitched outburst.

Jack shot back up to a standing position and after a brief moment of surprise, his face broke into a grin, complete with dimples, and that cute squinty-eyed smile she couldn't resist. He threw his arms wide in welcome. "I found you!"

She edged closer and the group of men moved aside while giving her curious looks. "What are you doing here?" she asked again.

His arms dropped but he crossed the few feet of space separating them so they didn't have to shout over the talking that had resumed around them. When he drew close he pulled an awkward leaning move as though he might hug her but then he didn't. Maybe she had pulled back, she wasn't certain. Either way, now they were standing there, between a group of American bros and a cranky bartender who was manning the small but packed bar beside the pool table.

She shook her head in a vain attempt to shake off the alcohol haze that was making rational thought impossible. If only she could take a moment to compose herself, to get her senses straight—to sober up a bit, at the very least. But he was here, now, standing right in front of her, mere inches away. And he smelled so *good*—a deliciously manly scent that had to be cologne or aftershave. No one smelled that good naturally.

He spoke first, distracting her from her mission to discover the source of his scent. "Are you okay?" he asked.

She peered up at him in confusion. "Why wouldn't I be okay? And what are you doing here?"

"I came to find you. Ivy sent me," he started.

Ice flooded her veins. Her mind instantly leapt to the worst possible scenario.

"Oh my God, Ivy. Is she okay? What's wrong? Is it the baby?"

Jack eyes widened in panic and he reached out to her before quickly pulling back. "No! No, no, she's fine. The baby's fine. Everybody is fine."

Holly slapped a hand over her heart, which had catapulted into double time in fear. Adrenaline coursed through her. "Don't scare me like," she snapped.

He took a step back. "Sorry, I didn't meant to—"

"If they're okay, why are you here?" She caught the bartender eyeing them with curiosity and lowered her voice.

A fresh wave of dizziness swept over her as her mind struggled to make sense of the fact that Jack Everett was in Paris, in her hostel…the man had developed one of the most successful gaming systems on the planet while still in college, she would bet everything she owned that he had never once stayed in a seedy hostel like this one.

Her eyes narrowed with suspicion. "How did you find me?"

He glanced side to side while giving her a wary look, like she might cause a scene. Oh no. Was that it? Was he here because of that night? Ivy's wedding night? She'd figured he'd be angry at the way it ended but she hadn't thought he would track her down in a foreign city just to confront her.

Their little corner between the bar and pool table was growing more crowded by the minute and she was pushed even closer to him by an elbow in the back.

"Ivy told me you'd probably be staying at a hostel in this neighborhood and this was my second try." He gave her his patented lopsided grin. "The guy behind the counter had no problem identifying a certain gorgeous blonde I know."

His tone was breezy and joking. For a split second, warmth radiated through her at the flirtatious way he was talking, but then she remembered that flirtatious was the way he talked with all women, all the time. She was nothing special. Crossing her arms over her chest and lifting her chin, she asked for what felt like the millionth time, "What. Are. You. Doing. Here?"

At her unpleasant tone, he dropped the flirty demeanor and she caught a glimpse of something—embarrassment maybe? He looked…sheepish.

Oh no. He *was* here about that night.

"Ivy sent me," he said again, this time looking a bit unsure of himself as he shifted from one foot to the other. "She was worried about you, being alone in the city and all."

Holly would have burst out laughing if she wasn't feeling so guilty about *that night*. As it was, she smothered a grin. Ivy, worried about her being in Paris alone? Aside from Oakdale, Paris was one of the safest places she'd ever lived and she'd been traveling on her own since she was eighteen. Her sister had ceased worrying about her about a decade ago.

The crowd around them was paying way too much attention to Jack. They both seemed to notice it at once. Jack, after all, was probably the equivalent of a superhero in the eyes of the tech nerds at the pool table— and just a plain old famous celebrity to everyone else. Holly shifted uncomfortably under the weight of their stares.

"Look, can we get out of here? I'd like to talk to you alone," Jack said. He leaned in so only she could hear and she held her breath to keep from losing her senses around that damned cologne.

She let him lead her out of the hostel by the arm as she fumbled in her muddled brain for a good explanation for that night—had anyone ever discovered a polite, believable way to nicely say, "It's not you, it's me?" The chilly night air was refreshing and helped to clear her head.

Holly took a couple of deep breaths as she followed him down the street. She needed to come up with a good reason for why she'd kissed him like that, let him touch her like that, made promises like that and then...run away.

Chapter 3

Two doors down from the hostel was a quiet café that suited Jack perfectly. So far Operation Rescue Holly was not going as planned. In fact, it was not going well—at all.

He hadn't expected her to be overjoyed to see him, not after the way he'd abandoned her like that after the wedding. He knew he owed her an apology but a month had passed, he was hoping she'd at least have cooled down a bit. But the woman who was glaring up at him at the hostel...that woman was red hot.

And sexy.

Nope. He was not going there. He'd made a promise to Ivy and Daniel, and himself, that he would treat this sweet, innocent young woman with the respect she deserved. He was all for fun and games with experienced women who knew how to play the game. But not someone kind and sweet and thoroughly innocent like his Holly.

Holly, just Holly, not *his* Holly.

He signaled to the waitress and when she came over he ordered a bottle of wine. This conversation would require some assistance of the alcohol variety. Holly had been oddly quiet since they left the hostel and now she leaned back in her seat across from nibbling on her lower lip with a decidedly wary look in her eyes.

She was probably waiting for him to apologize. He cleared his throat a bit and that seemed to bring her to life. She leaned forward so her elbows were on the table and she fixed her gaze directly on him. He tried not to notice the way her V-neck T-shirt inched down, revealing just a hint of cleavage. She raked her hair back and her blond curls spilled over her shoulders in a haphazard way—he had a momentary flash of what she would look like in bed in the morning with tousled hair and a sleepy smile.

But she was not smiling now and her blue eyes were terrifyingly direct. She seemed to see everything about him. Was it his imagination or was she looking into his soul?

Okay, now he was officially psyching himself out. *Be a man and apologize already.* He sat up a little straighter in his chair. "Look, Holly, I just—"

At the same time, Holly started, "Jack, I think I owe—"

They stopped and shared an awkward laugh.

The waitress arrived with their bottle of wine and they waited in silence as she poured two glasses. Jack all but lunged for his when she was done.

When she walked away he tried again. "I'm sorry I left you that night."

"I'm so sorry I ran away that night," Holly blurted out at the same time.

He was sure his look of surprise matched the wide-eyed shocked on Holly's face as they each registered what the other had said.

"Wait, what?" he said.

"You left *me*?" Holly repeated.

They stared at one another again. She ran away? So she hadn't been waiting for him to come to her bed that night? All this time he'd been picturing her lying there on the bed, perhaps naked, depending on the particular daydream, waiting for him to return once he'd gotten protection but she—

"You never came back that night?" He couldn't tell if she sounded angry or amused. Or both.

He shook his head. He opened his mouth to speak but was stuck on where to begin. How to explain that he had never wanted a woman more than he'd wanted her that night. The kiss they'd shared had been so hot, she was so passionate. But the moment he'd stepped out of her guest room at the villa and into the bracing night air, the reality of what he was about to do hit him. He was going to seduce his friend's sister, a sweet, innocent young woman who'd had too much champagne and was high on wedding romance. He knew he couldn't go through with it no matter how badly he wanted her. "I had a crisis of conscience," he said. One of her brows arched mockingly and he added, "You weren't waiting for me?"

She shook her head and her lips were twitching upward. Amusement seemed to be winning out. "I guess you could call it a crisis of conscience."

Their eyes met again and this time they both burst out laughing.

"So you're not mad at me then?" he asked.

She shook her head. "Not as long as you're not mad at me."

He reached a hand out across the table to shake on it. "Friends?"

She slipped her hand into his to shake on it and he knew then he'd made a mistake. The touch of her warm little hand was all it took to be overwhelmed with awareness of this woman. She jerked her hand back quickly. Had she felt it too?

They sipped their wine for a moment and then she looked up at him with an adorable little wiggle of her nose. "Hey Jack, what *are* you doing here?"

* * * *

Holly watched Jack toy with his wine glass. Comprehension dawned— Mister Too Cool for School was actually nervous. She'd thought he was here to here to give her hell for running away on him but now she was even more intrigued. She leaned over the table and caught his eye.

"If Ivy and the baby are okay…" she prompted.

"Well, uh," he paused as a steaming tray filled with entrees passed by their table. "Are you hungry? I'm hungry. I'm going to grab us some menus."

"Um, okay," she drawled. She wasn't trying to be rude, but really, finding the guy she'd jilted a month earlier in a foreign city, in her hostel of all places…well, it was a tad disconcerting.

She was still coming to grips with the fact that he hadn't returned to her bedroom that night. She could still feel the nervous anticipation as he'd walked out of the bedroom, promising in that sexy voice of his that he would be right back. She was lying there, clothed but thoroughly disheveled, and more turned on than she'd ever been in her entire life. She had been so excited for what was to come—and then it had happened. Panic struck. The sound of her heartbeat warred with the whirring of the overhead fan. She'd landed in the world of reality with a thud and she was overwhelmed. And then she did what she'd always done best. She ran.

And all this time she'd thought that he'd come back to her room only to find an empty bed and her favorite pair of earrings that she'd accidentally left behind. But no, he had left her there. What if she hadn't fled? She would have lain there for hours wondering what had happened, what had gone wrong…maybe she *should* be pissed.

She tried to cling to the anger but she couldn't make it stick. It seemed the height of hypocrisy to be angry with him for something she'd done as well. Still, she couldn't help but feel a little hurt, whether it was rational or not.

She watched Jack trying to get the waitress's attention. He still hadn't answered her. Had he really come all this way to apologize?

Ugh, that was equally embarrassing and sweet.

Or maybe…maybe he was just looking for an excuse to see her again. Maybe he hadn't been able to stop thinking about her either. What if he too had been fantasizing about that night, wondering what would have happened if they'd seen it through. If they hadn't run.

She had a flash of his hands on her, caressing her through the gown as his lips moved over her neck, her shoulders. Maybe he'd spent the past month reliving that night too. A wave of heat coursed through her, so intense her mouth went dry.

She took a sip of the wine. She should probably eat some dinner before she drank much more.

The waitress handed them their menus and it was all Holly could do to concentrate on the words. Her mind couldn't seem to focus; it was too busy obsessing over the man sitting across from her. When the server came back to take their order, Holly picked the first item that caught her eye and handed back the menu.

Alone once more and without the distraction of food, Holly and Jack squared off. Holly forced a smile despite the butterflies that threatened to overtake her stomach. If there was one thing she knew how to do it was fake confidence no matter how bizarre the situation. "So tell me, Jack, you didn't really come to my hostel just to apologize, did you?"

One side of his mouth turned up in a grin that made the atmosphere seem a million times thinner. There was not nearly enough oxygen in this restaurant. He'd been thinking of her, too. That was it. He had come after her. She couldn't name the emotion that was wreaking havoc with her senses, making it difficult to breathe or see or hear. It was excitement and fear and lust and nerves all rolled into one.

"So the reason I'm here," he started. "Your sister did send me. Er, I mean, I offered to come here on your sister's behalf…."

Jack's awkwardness made Holly's anxiety increase a million times over. Toying with the napkin in her lap, her voice came out sharper than she intended. "Just spit it out."

"Benjamin's conference is in Paris, Texas, not Paris, France."

Holly's blood ran cold at Benjamin's name coming out of Jack's mouth. She sat in stunned silence for a moment as the rest of his words made their way to her fuzzy brain. Guilt was the first emotion to deliver a sucker punch. Here she'd been daydreaming about Jack while she was supposed to be hunting down her soon-to-be fiancé for a romantic surprise. What kind of almost girlfriend did that make her? A terrible one.

And then the rest of the sentence clicked into place in Holly's brain. Humiliation washed over her in a tidal wave. She struggled to catch her breath. Oh no. Not only was she an idiot of the first order but this man—Jack Everett, of all people—knew it. He knew that she was here chasing after the man she couldn't even call boyfriend. How much had Ivy told him?

"Oh God," she muttered. She picked up her glass and took a gulp of wine.

When she set it down she found Jack watching her with...ugh, was that pity? That was not acceptable.

She took another large sip of wine and forced a grin. "Guess that's what I get for being romantic," she quipped. "So how did Ivy know that—"

"Your mom."

"Right, of course." She'd never fully understood the desire to be swallowed up by the ground until that moment.

Jack picked up a fork and toyed with it. "Ivy wasn't sure when you would call again or check your emails and she didn't want you running all over Paris on a wild goose chase."

Holly had to laugh at that. That was exactly how she'd describe her day. She'd been on a wild goose chase to find a wannabe boyfriend who wasn't there. Jack seemed to loosen up considerably when she laughed. He was grinning at her as he reached for his glass. He was probably just relieved she hadn't burst into tears at the news.

"Thank you," she forced herself to say. "For going out of your way to save me from..." Save her from, what? Herself? Heat rose to her cheeks. There was no sign of pity in his eyes but she was certain she felt it oozing from him under the guise of good intentions.

"No problem, it wasn't out of my way."

"Well, I guess it was my good luck that you were in Paris during my time of need."

She forced a smile. He was lying. She wasn't sure how she knew but it was obvious. He was a good liar but she was better. She'd been able to see through his charming little white lies from the first moment they'd met, when he'd introduced himself to her at the rehearsal dinner. He'd told her he loved weddings and she'd called him out on the lie.

She almost called him out on this lie but stopped herself. She appreciated the lie for what it was—he was trying to make her feel less pathetic.

Nice try. The reality of her situation was slowly sinking in and she tried not to let the horror show on her face. Her stomach roiled and for a moment, she thought she might be sick. She had blown so much money to come here and it was all for nothing. Plus, she'd missed out on another chance to win Benjamin over. And now, all the world—well, her family and Jack, at least—had witnessed her desperation. And that's what it was.

Maggie Dallen

Desperation. Up until that point she had been able to convince herself that it was a romantic gesture but now...

"Are you all right?" Jack asked.

Holly's head jerked in a nod and she took another sip of wine. The waitress set down some bread and she lunged for it. She needed to sober up otherwise she would never be able to control the emotions that were threatening to eat her alive.

"So this Benjamin guy—" Jack started.

Holly winced. "I'd rather not talk about it." She was embarrassed enough, the last thing she wanted to do was talk about her infatuation with Benjamin...and certainly not with Jack, of all people.

"Fair enough," Jack said. "But I really am glad I got an excuse to see you...."

Truth. She could be a human lie detector around this guy.

"I'm glad we had a chance to clear the air about...that night," he finished.

That night. There it was again, larger than life in her mind, like an incredibly vivid dream that lingers long after you wake.

"Me too," she said. "I mean, we're going to be seeing so much of each other."

"Right, between Danny and Ivy and now the new baby, we'll be seeing each other all the time." Holly's heart rate picked up speed. He was right. There was no escaping it. Jack would be a constant in her life.

He looked so eager to make things right, to make her happy, that she went along with the jovial attitude. "At major holidays and life events, at the very least," she agreed.

"Right. So I'm glad we had a chance to clear the air," he said again.

She forced a bright smile. "And thank God we didn't...you know."

He blinked at her in surprise for a moment before quickly agreeing with her a little too wholeheartedly. "Yeah, I mean...yes. Absolutely. So true. That would have made things really...complicated."

"And awkward," she added.

He nodded as he reached for the cheese plate the waitress set down. "Oh definitely. So awkward."

She told herself she should not be offended that he was so enthusiastically happy they didn't have sex. She'd said it first, after all. But still. His eager agreement wasn't exactly good for her ego.

She raised her glass, "To the best mistake we ever avoided."

He clinked his glass against hers, "Amen to that."

* * * *

The relief Jack felt at having gotten the apology off his chest was tempered by the fact that it had apparently been completely unnecessary. *She* had left *him*.

He watched her tear apart the bread and shove a piece in her mouth. He didn't know whether he should be relieved or angry. Though he was glad he hadn't hurt her feelings, his ego was more than a little bruised. He had been so sure she was into it—into *him*. He thought they'd had something special that night and now it turned out she'd run away from him as soon as his back was turned.

The waitress headed toward them with steaming plates of food and Holly's eyes lit up like a kid in a candy store. She was more beautiful than he'd remembered. He'd started to think he was exaggerating her charms, but then he'd spotted her in the dingy hostel. His memory hadn't done her justice. No picture or mere memory could capture her larger-than-life charisma or her zest for life. She practically glowed with an innate joy, a youthful excitement that had nothing to do with age and everything to do with the way she viewed the world around her.

And then there was the fact that she was just plain hot. She had killer curves, wild blond curls, and big blue eyes…eyes that were currently ogling the meat and cheese selection the waitress set before them.

Everything about this woman screamed sweetness and light. She was the type of woman you take home to meet the family. She was clearly long-term girlfriend material, it was no wonder she'd run from him that night. Isn't that why he'd fled as well? They both knew that she deserved better than him.

The food had arrived just in time. He was starting to think of ways to bring up Benjamin again but he was saved by the distraction that food provided. He didn't know how much he really wanted to hear about this other man. Clearly Holly had feelings for the guy but did he really need to hear the details?

Ivy didn't like Benjamin, that's all he needed to know. Ivy had good judgment in men—after all, she just married one of his best friends. If she didn't think Benjamin was good enough for her sister, neither did he.

Of course, Ivy hadn't come out and *said* she didn't like him but he knew his friend well and it was obvious that she had her misgivings. That was good enough for Jack to thoroughly dislike him.

He knew how to scare off other men and, even better, he was an expert in the art of distraction. He would just have to take Holly's mind off of the loser so she could find someone worthy of her awesomeness.

All the better that he'd come here himself. Even though "here" was Paris, a city he'd been avoiding for the last few years, ever since his brother and sister-in-law moved here for Robbie's new job.

He couldn't think about Robbie right now. Things had gotten so strained between him and his older brother that he didn't know where to begin to make things right.

But Holly—he could make things right for her.

She looked up then, as if just realizing that there was a world beyond the food on her plate. She was adorable when she was voracious. A bit frightening, but adorable.

"I was really hungry," she mumbled around a mouthful of food, a slightly sheepish look on her face.

"Feel better?" he asked.

She rolled her eyes in ecstasy. "Much." He refilled their wine glasses as Holly settled back in her seat, clearly more at ease now that she was fed.

"So how long have you been in Paris?" she asked.

He fiddled with the fork on his plate. "I just got here today," he said. He knew where this was going.

Her brows furrowed together as she studied him and he was uncomfortably aware of the intensity of her stare. Why did he have the feeling she could see right through him?

Her eyes narrowed. "Wait, you didn't come all the way to Paris just to find me, did you?"

He opened his mouth to say no but stopped with his mouth open. Somehow he knew she would see right through his lie.

"Yes," he admitted.

He thought for a moment that she would ask why but she didn't. Perhaps she was just as averse to rehashing their apology conversation. He figured neither of them came out looking great in that debacle.

"I'd assumed you were here for business. Or for pleasure, maybe." Her voice was soft and for a moment her eyes didn't meet his. There was a vulnerability there that he'd never seen before. She looked... embarrassed. Or hurt, maybe. The expression was there and gone so quickly he wondered if he imagined it. Then her gaze met his again and for one crazy moment he was certain she could see everything—every lie he'd told, every friend he'd let down, every heart he'd broken.

Her next question cut into that disturbing train of thought. "Do you like Paris?" she asked. Her head was cocked to the side and he again had the uncomfortable sensation that she would see through any lie or evasion.

He let out a sigh, "Not really, no."

Her eyes widened in surprise but she didn't give him a hard time, which he appreciated. Most people he knew would try to sell him on the romantic city's illustrious charms or go on and on about the amazing food. He knew all of that. His aversion to the city had nothing to do with the city itself.

She surprised him with a wide grin that made his groin ache in recognition. Jesus, that smile was magnetic.

"So you just came to find little ol' me?" she teased with an over the top southern accent. "Much obliged, I'm sure."

He pretended to tip an imaginary cowboy hat. "My pleasure, little lady."

Her giggle made him think of sunshine and rainbows and hot air balloons. This woman was sweeter than candy.

He leaned across the table; he needed to be closer to her like he needed oxygen. "Brunelli would like you to stay at his apartment in the city. He insists."

She shook her head and her curls bounced around her shoulders. "Tell Brunelli thanks, but no thanks. I'm fine at the hostel."

He wanted to push the issue. The hostel was not what anyone would call clean, and he had little confidence that it was a safe place for anyone on their own, let alone a beautiful woman. But pride was obvious in the set of her jaw and her stiff posture. The last thing he wanted was to come across as the spoiled rich guy who tossed around phrases like "my private jet" just to impress. If she wanted to stay in the dingy hostel, that was up to her, whether he liked it or not. And he did *not* like it.

"Fine," he said, as he hailed the waitress for the check. "But at the very least let me walk you home so I know you get there safe."

Chapter 4

Holly had to admit—it was rather nice being with someone so chivalrous. She was just as progressive as the next woman but it was oddly sweet—and totally foreign—to be treated like such a lady. Jack paid their tab and helped her into her jacket. He held the door for her on the way out and even insisted on walking her all the way inside the hostel. She was pretty sure he would have walked her all the way to her room if they hadn't been stopped by the sound of a man's voice calling her name from the bar area in the back.

"Holly! Holly, is that you?" the voice called in a heavy French accent.

Oh no. She knew that voice. For the second time that night, a voice from her past cut through the music in the bar. This could not be happening....again.

Holly tried to make a beeline toward the hall leading to her room, with Jack close on her heels. "Is that guy talking to you?" he asked.

"Who?" She kept walking but the Frenchman calling her name was faster than his large frame would suggest. He stepped into her path, causing Holly to stop so suddenly that Jack collided into her back.

"Holly," the man said again, before pulling her into an embrace.

For a moment she was trapped between the solid wall of a man who was hugging her and Jack, who was still close behind her.

For the love of all things holy, why did she have to run into Lyon now?

"What are you doing back in France?" he asked. Lyon, her ex-lover, was sweet in a big oaf sort of way and he looked exactly the same as she remembered him with his leather biker jacket and long, black hair.

"I, uh, I'm just here for a short visit," she said. She saw Lyon's eyes light up in an all too familiar look and she remembered with vivid clarity just how hard it had been to disentangle herself from this emotional, needy biker. So she added, "With my boyfriend."

She didn't turn to see Jack's expression when she reached out and clasped his hand. The childish move did the trick. The hopeful look in the Frenchman's eyes flickered and died as quickly as it was ignited.

"Too bad," he said, eyeing Jack in a not-so-friendly manner.

He turned back to Holly, effectively dismissing Jack from the conversation. "You look good, *ma chérie.*"

Jack, apparently not intimidated by the brick wall before him, took a step forward and slid an arm around Holly's shoulders. He stuck his hand out, "Glad to meet you, I'm her *boyfriend*, Jack." Holly doubted anyone in the vicinity could have missed the not-so-subtle way he stressed the word "boyfriend."

Lyon shook Jack's hand while giving him a doubtful look and Holly smothered a grin. Lyon was hot but not the sharpest tool in the shed. He mumbled his name before turning back to Holly.

"I have to get back to work. Come find me if you want to grab a drink."

Holly smiled and made a vague noise of agreement. There was no way she would be going down that path again, thank you very much. He was exactly the kind of guy she was trying to avoid. No more flings for her, thank you very much. She was ready for the real deal.

Lyon walked away with a sorry slump in his shoulders. Before Holly could turn to thank Jack for going along with her lie, they were distracted by three very drunk girls heading toward them with three men in tow, each more obnoxious than the next.

They moved past Holly and Jack to one of the rooms down the hall and a few seconds later the sound of a stereo cranked up to the highest volume came blaring out of one of the rooms.

"Are those…" Jack started.

"My roommates?" Holly finished. "Yup."

They stood side by side for a moment, listening to the music blaring from the room and the loud shrieks of laughter followed by a booming male voice declaring, "That's how we *do!*"

Jack leaned over so he could talk directly into her ear. "Do you think perhaps you may want to reconsider Brunelli's offer?"

Holly glanced over to see his smug, charming grin a little too close for comfort. "Give me one minute to grab my bag."

* * * *

"So, are you going to tell me who that guy was?" Jack asked as they strolled through the winding, cobblestone streets leading toward Brunelli's apartment.

Holly glanced over at him with a wide-eyed innocent look. "Oh, just someone I met when I was here a couple of summers ago."

"Oh, come on. I just risked my life pretending to be your boyfriend back there," he said.

She turned to him with a wicked grin. "How does it feel being on the other side of the charade?"

He had to laugh at that. What were the odds that he would find himself pretending to be in a couple...again. And with Ivy's sister, no less. "Okay, fine," he said, "I guess I did have that coming. But you've got to admit. I did come to your rescue in a time of need—the least you can do is give me the dirt. How did you two meet?"

He was more curious than he cared to admit. This woman, who looked like an angel who had fallen straight out of heaven—hell, her hair even looked like a halo under the streetlamps—was definitely not a saint. And that dichotomy was extremely...intriguing.

He thought she was ignoring him but it seemed she was only lost in the memory for a moment. When she spoke, her tone was whimsical. "He picked me up on his motorcycle."

He nearly tripped over his own feet. "Excuse me?"

She gave him a sidelong look of amusement—clearly he hadn't succeeded in hiding his surprise. "I was hitchhiking from Nice to Paris and Lyon picked me up."

He found himself scowling at her and the voice that came out of his mouth sounded absurdly like his father's. "So you just got on the back of a bike of a complete stranger?" Hating himself for how stodgy he sounded, he still couldn't stop from adding, "A stranger who looked like *that*?"

"Like what?" she asked, again all innocence. But she was clearly laughing at him, the twinkle in her eye was not from the wine. Well, maybe it was a little from the wine, she *was* walking a little...crooked.

Jack shoved his hands in his pockets and stared straight ahead. He would not be his father, the square. Or worse, his brother, the square of all squares. "So you two shared a cozy ride on his Harley—"

"It was an Avinton motorcycle," she corrected.

"You shared a ride on his *bike*," he said. "And what, you rode off into the sunset?"

"More like, we rode to the nearest biker bar," she said. Her eyes crinkled up in the most adorable way when she was laughing at him. "And then we took the scenic route to the city."

She got that dreamy nostalgic look on her face again and it irritated the hell out of him. "But true love didn't last, I take it."

She outright laughed at that. "It was hardly love. It was more like…lust."

Jack had to force his feet to keep moving, one in front of the other. He was overcome with the simultaneous urge to head back to the hostel to pummel the giant biker and spin her into his arms to kiss her silly. The word "lust" coming from those lips, that mouth…he wanted her to lust after *him*.

No he didn't. Come back to reality, son. This is Holly Sinclair you're talking to, sister to one of your best friends. Although at that moment, Ivy and Daniel seemed very far away. In another galaxy. Would it really be so bad to taste the forbidden fruit? After all, she wasn't a sheltered innocent from Ohio as he'd assumed. She was wild, adventurous…passionate.

So then why the hell had she run away from him that night?

"He hooked me up with a job waitressing at the club where he was a bouncer," she continued.

"How sweet," Jack muttered.

She ignored him. "We had a lot of fun that summer but…."

"But?"

She gave him a rueful look and shook her head. "It ended. Story over."

"Aw, what kind of ending is that?" He honestly wanted to hear her bad-talk her ex. What was wrong with him? *He was jealous.* No, that couldn't be right. He didn't do jealousy. He was not a jealous guy. He was laid back, he was cool, he was….

"You were amazing back there," Holly said.

He looked over to see her grinning at him, a mischievous look on her face. "Not many men would step up and pretend to be my boyfriend in that scenario."

"Any man would love to be your boyfriend, pretend or otherwise," he said.

She rolled her eyes at the flattery. "I'm serious. I mean, most guys I know would run in the opposite direction if they were being glared at by a guy like that."

"A guy like what?" he asked, feigning ignorance.

"A guy who's built like a brick wall," she said dryly.

He pretended to ponder her statement. "You're right," he said. "You owe me."

Her laughter was light and musical. "How am I ever going to repay you?" she teased. Her voice had gone soft and sultry and it had an instantaneous effect on his groin. She was flirting with him and it was completely irresistible.

This woman would be the end of him.

Before he could answer the provocative question, she continued, "I suppose I'll just have to do the same for you."

"Pretend to be my boyfriend?"

She swatted his arm but ignored the comment. "I imagine you have loads of history in this city, am I right? You must have some serious baggage here. I mean, why else would anyone hate this city?"

Jack thought of his brother who he'd barely spoken to in three years. He supposed you could call that baggage, although it was more like a giant U-Haul of unresolved issues.

She took his silence for a yes. "I knew it." She turned so she was walking backward and could look him square in the face. "I bet you've left behind a trail of women with broken hearts. I'm surprised they even allow you into the country, you're probably a wanted man."

She was teasing, he knew she was teasing, but for the first time in his life, he hated the playboy image he'd created for himself. But there was no way he was going to tell this woman the humiliating stories behind his fall out with his brother. When it came down to being seen as a player or a fool, he'd take player every time. He forced a smile and threw his hands up in surrender. "You caught me."

Laughing, she went to turn back around so she was facing forward but her heel caught on a cobblestone. Jack caught her just in time. She was pressed against him and he could smell her soft, warm scent—a heady mix of vanilla and some sort of flower. Her breasts were soft against his chest. She was so close, he could feel her breath on his cheeks and his arms closed tight around her.

He couldn't let go.

Surprise left her mouth slightly open and her eyes wide as she looked up at him. Her lips were so close. He could remember with vivid clarity that passionate kiss they'd shared at the wedding. It had been next to impossible to drag himself away from her then. He didn't know if he could do it again. If he kissed her now, there was no going back. He wanted her in his arms...in his bed.

She was the one who put an end to the moment, pulling back roughly and shaking her head as if to shake off the thick tension that had developed between them.

"So how far is this place?" she asked, her voice just a bit too loud.

She'd felt it too. And she was walking away from it.

"Are you sure you know where we're going?" she continued.

Jack followed her lead. "I was there earlier today to drop off my bags. We're close, I promise," he said, continuing to walk and pretending that nothing had happened. Easier said than done given the thick desire that had him struggling to think straight.

He latched on to the last topic of conversation. "So we have a deal then," he said, doing his part to get them back on track. "If I find myself entangled in a, uh, *sticky situation* with an ex-lover...."

"I'll come to your rescue," Holly finished. She held out her little finger. "Pinky swear."

He led her around the corner and pointed triumphantly at the apartment complex ahead of them. "M'lady, may I welcome you to... Brunelli's home."

The concierge on duty was expecting them since Jack had already made himself at home at the plush pad. He gestured for them to take the private elevator and they rode in silence to the penthouse suite.

The doors slid open silently, revealing the spacious, opulent apartment in a rather dramatic manner. Holly's gasp of pleasure made him ridiculously happy.

"Make yourself at home. Brunelli insists," he said.

He started to give her the grand tour but he hadn't gotten far before she was racing ahead of him, throwing open doors and exclaiming over every little luxury. All of the stuff that he'd come to take for granted over the years, ever since he'd first come into serious money.

Making money came easily to him—but holding on to it was another matter. It hadn't taken him long to make back the fortune he'd so easily lost during his first shot at the big leagues. Learning from his past mistakes, he'd surrounded himself with people far more reliable than him and reveled in the glitzy lifestyle secure in the knowledge that his business partners wouldn't let him repeat his past mistakes.

Jack trusted himself as little as Robbie did, maybe less—but he did trust Daniel and Brunelli and it was a relief to know that the employees of EverTech were safe from his curse.

Some people had a way of turning everything they touched to gold— like Danny, for instance—Jack, on the other hand had the unique ability to turn everything he touched to dust. He was a bull in a china shop when it came to life. Every ex-girlfriend would attest to that, not to mention his family and friends. Even those who loved him most openly admitted that he couldn't be trusted. Not with anything that mattered, at least, and certainly not with anything involving a commitment.

Holly raced through the kitchen ahead of him, on her way to the wing that housed the master bedroom, her squeals of excitement echoing down the hall and drawing him out of his walk down self-pity lane.

He followed Holly's excited voice and laughed aloud at her exuberance. Jack had grown accustomed to the blasé attitudes of the wealthy elite he was surrounded by these days and Holly's reaction was refreshing. It made him feel like he was experiencing first-class living for the first time.

Jack caught up to her in the entrance to the master bathroom, where her mouth was literally hanging open in shock at the brilliant gold and marble opulence.

He grabbed her hand and gave it a tug. "Come on, you haven't seen the best part yet." He led her through the apartment to the back living room and through the sliding doors.

Holly let out a little squeak of pleasure at the sight before her. Paris, in all its glory. Lights twinkling across the Seine, the Eiffel Tower illuminated against the night sky.

"It's like a movie," she whispered.

Despite the view ahead of him, he couldn't take his eyes off of her. It was physically impossible to tear his eyes away from the sheer joy in those incredible eyes.

* * * *

It was magic. For the second time in her life, Holly felt like she was in a fairy tale. Was it this man or was it romantic settings where they seemed to find themselves? First a wedding in Tuscany, and now, on the balcony of a penthouse suite in Paris.

But she'd been in plenty of exotic, romantic destinations and she'd never felt like Cinderella before.

It was Jack. He was larger than life, like a hero from a comic book. Kind and handsome, intelligent and playful, sexy and…charming. She nearly laughed aloud at the realization—she felt like Cinderella because he was a real life Prince Charming.

She kept her eyes trained on the amazing display of lights before her but every sense was tuned in to the man beside her. He was watching her. She could feel his gaze move over her like a caress.

He wanted her.

The thought made her so hot, her insides seemed to melt. She needed air. Shedding her jacket, she inhaled deeply and ordered her body to calm down. This was ridiculous. She was standing outside on a cool summer's eve and yet she couldn't seem to catch her breath.

Had he moved closer or was it just her imagination? He seemed too close, she couldn't think straight.

"Holly." Her name sounded like a question and a statement all at once. He moved just a little closer. Close enough for her to feel his warmth and smell his light, intoxicating cologne. She turned toward him and felt his hand brush against her waist.

That was all it took. That slight touch broke down the physical barrier between them and she was in his arms as if it was the most natural thing in the world. Like they were a couple who had been dancing together for decades and moved into place out of habit. He was gazing down at her but he was backlit by the sliding doors and his eyes were in shadows.

One of his arms was wrapped around her waist and he moved his free arm around her back so she was imprisoned against him. They stood that way for a moment, frozen in an embrace. His head was tipped toward her and she was gazing up at him. The air was too thick to breathe.

She couldn't see his eyes but she could feel his stare on her lips. Nervous excitement made her lightheaded as she waited. What was he waiting for? Her lips parted for air and she heard his soft groan.

She couldn't have moved if she wanted to once he started to lower his head toward hers. His lips were strong and hard against hers as he crushed her against him. This was nothing like the sweet, torturously teasing kiss at the wedding, with its promise of a slow seduction. This was passion.

Her mind went blank as sensations wreaked havoc on her sanity. She met him kiss for kiss with an urgency that was almost overwhelming. White-hot heat coursed through her as his lips moved against hers, their tongues tangling, almost battling in the most intensely passionate kiss she'd ever experienced.

He stroked her back with one hand, the heat of his touch cutting through the thin cotton of her blouse. With gentle pressure, he held her even closer and she wrapped her arms around his neck, clinging tighter, trying to slake the aching desire that was bordering on painful.

She wanted him everywhere, she wanted him *inside of* her.

The hand on her back moved up, through her curls to cup the back of her neck, his thumb brushing against the base of her throat in an intimate gesture. She let out a moan of pleasure as his other hand moved from her waist to the side of her breast, tantalizingly close to where she needed his touch but still teasing her.

He pulled back his head just enough to lean his forehead against hers to give them a moment to catch their breath. His voice was low and husky with desire when he muttered, "God, Holly, you're so beautiful. I'm so glad I found you."

Found her? A distant part of her brain echoed the words. What did he mean, "found her?"

Thoughts slowly started to form through the haze of desire and sluggishly clicked into place like puzzle pieces. Jack had come here to find her. To save her. Because she'd gone to the wrong Paris. For Benjamin.

Benjamin.

Her stomach plummeted. Oh God, she was going to hell. Pulling back from his embrace with more strength than grace, she turned away from Jack in horror.

"I can't do this." She'd meant to speak the words but they came out in a harsh whisper. She was supposed to be here to win Benjamin and instead she was in another man's arms? What was wrong with her?

Jack stared at her wide-eyed. He was still holding his arms out toward her but dropped them abruptly and ran a hand through his mussed hair. He let out a loud exhale. "Yeah, of course. Sorry if I…" his voice trailed off and he made an awkward gesture in her general direction.

Holly shook her head. "You didn't."

She should explain her actions. She knew that but her brain was having a hard time formulating sentences.

This was agony. Her body was screaming for completion and Jack was right there. It took every ounce of willpower to maintain that distance. He was hovering near the doorway. *Why did he have to look so good?* With his shirt partially unbuttoned—*had she done that?*—his disheveled hair and a five o'clock shadow, he was sexy as hell.

It was like he was *trying* to make this difficult for her. She backed up a few more steps and braced herself against the railing for support. Her legs were still trembling and the throbbing heat at her core had barely subsided.

He started backing away toward the balcony door. "I, uh…oh hell, I need a cold shower," he said with a humorless laugh as he ducked back into the apartment.

She let out a long breath she hadn't realized she'd been holding. She could breathe again now that he was not in kissing distance. She collapsed into one of the chairs on the patio and took several deep, steadying breaths.

What had she done? Guilt gnawed at her stomach. She had come all this way for a grand romantic gesture and ended up in the arms of another. She laughed bitterly in the darkness. *Well done, Holly.*

For the first time all night the reality of her situation struck her. She had flown to France to surprise the man she loved—and he wasn't there! Now she really did start to laugh as her eyes filled with tears of self-pity. The whole thing was ludicrous.

She propped her feet up on an end table and let her head fall back against the back of the chair. She made a game of trying to find stars in the night sky, not an easy feat with all the lights from the city spread out below her.

After a little while, the anxious pit in her stomach subsided and her brain was clear once again. Her body was still a bundle of sensitive nerve endings thanks to that kiss but she was no longer aching in all out agony.

What would Benjamin say when he found out? Not about the kiss. There was no reason to confess to that. For all she knew, he was shacking up with some Paris, Texas floozy right now. That thought only managed to bring back the pit in her stomach.

She'd been in a battle for his affection for the past six months—or at least that's how it felt. First it was a battle to help him overcome any lingering feelings for his ex, then she'd struggled to make him see that she was capable of settling down—that she could be the stable, reliable woman he needed. And now she'd gone and proven to him that she's just as flaky as ever by running ever off to another continent on a whim.

Love shouldn't be this hard.

A wave of exhaustion washed over her and it had nothing to do with the wine or running all over Paris. She was tired of trying to make things work with Benjamin. What more did she need to do to make him see that they were meant to be together? A flicker of doubt shot through her. *Maybe it was time to give up.*

Her chest tightened in pain at the mere thought. An image of the life they could have—of the *family* they could have—filled her mind. The dream she'd been harboring ever since that terrible night when she'd lost her baby washed away the uncertainty. The hope of the family to come was what drove her, it was everything. No way was she giving up on that dream. She just needed to find a way to get through to Benjamin, to make him realize once and for all that she was serious about their relationship.

And Jack? He was a remnant of her past, a living reminder of the lifestyle and choices she was leaving behind.

Chapter 5

Jack woke late the next day. He'd tossed and turned all night in a miserable attempt to sleep, thanks to his irresistible new roommate and their late night make out session that had ended far too soon, as far as he was concerned. *But it was for the best.*

There was no sign of Holly when he woke so he made his way to the kitchen to scour the pantry for some coffee. He was glad Holly had ended things when she had, he told himself for the fifteenth time since waking. She was his best friend's sister which meant she was off limits. Besides, she was in love with another man, which meant she was really, *really* off-limits.

That thought should have been a relief. It meant that he was in no danger of hurting her heart, just like she'd been completely unfazed by their kiss at the wedding. He should be happy. Instead he found himself scowling at a nearly empty pantry, which was how Holly found him a minute later.

"Did that peanut butter do something to offend you?" he heard her ask from the kitchen doorway.

He glanced over and quickly looked away. Dammit. She looked hot as hell in an oversized T-shirt with tousled hair and no makeup. She looked like she'd just come from bed.

He sucked in a deep breath at the vivid image of her lying naked in his bed. Was it too early for another cold shower? He shut the pantry door a little too loudly. "Hey," he said. He couldn't think of anything else to say. *Him.* Jake Everett. A man who had a retort for everything, a witty aside for any time of day. But this morning, when he needed his wits most? *Hey.* That was all he could come up with.

She gave him a little smirk that had him half convinced she could read his mind as she sidled past him to grab an apple from the fruit bowl. "Please tell me there's coffee."

She leaned against the counter beside him, so close he could feel the heat from her skin. So close he could touch her if he so desired. And oh, he desired.

Pushing himself away from the counter he strode to the other side of the kitchen as though pillaging the almost bare fridge was an urgent matter. "Sorry," he said. "No coffee." He turned to see her pursing her lips in a comically exaggerated scowl.

"Well, that just won't do," she said, tossing the apple onto the counter. She whirled off toward the bedroom she'd claimed the night before and called over her shoulder, "Throw some clothes on, Everett, we're going out."

He threw a jacket over his T-shirt and jeans and was surprised to find her already waiting by the door, her wild curls thrown up into a messy bun and clad in simple jeans and the same oversized-T, which, he now noticed, sported a faded band logo with an illegible autograph.

He raised a questioning brow and nodded to the name. "Big fan?"

One side of her mouth curved up in a saucy grin. "I was that night."

Struck dumb for the second time that morning, Jack could only watch in wide-eyed wonder as she swung around, her massive tote nearly knocking him over as she led the way out the door.

* * * *

They found a tiny café a couple of blocks away and Jack watched Holly take her first sip with eyes closed while letting out a loud moan of ecstasy. She opened her eyes when he laughed. "What's so funny?" she asked.

She was smiling at him and her face was fresh-scrubbed and makeup-less. He was sure she'd never looked more beautiful.

"You are," he said, taking a sip of his own brew. He let out a contented sigh, which made her laugh in return. She held her mug up to cheers his.

"To coffee," she said.

"No," he said in an exaggerated French accent. "To *café*."

She feigned a serious look to match his and echoed, "To *café*."

She linked her arm through his in a friendly, almost sisterly way as they walked back down the street, neither apparently in much of a hurry to return to the scene of the crime, as he was beginning to think of last night's epic make out session.

They were walking the opposite way from the apartment, toward the Seine.

"So how long do I have?" she asked.

"To live?" he teased.

She rolled her eyes at the lame joke. "In Paris. When do we have to head back?"

He looked at her in surprise. "I thought you wanted to see Ivy."

Her eyes widened in offense and shock. "Of course I do! I just—" She stopped talking abruptly and her lips pursed to the side in a chagrined look.

"You just…" he repeated.

She shook her head and gave him a sidelong glance. "I'm not exactly excited to show up…like this."

She didn't explain but she didn't have to. "Like this" was having been found in the wrong Paris. Chasing after a guy. An unexpected wave of annoyance made his voice sharper than he intended. "I take it she doesn't approve of Benjamin?"

Her brows drew together in confusion. "I don't need her *approval.*"

So she basically admitted it. Ivy didn't like him which meant, he wasn't good enough, which meant….what? He could go for it? He wasn't sure that logic would stand up to Daniel's standards.

"It's just embarrassing is all," Holly said with a sigh.

He looked down at the top of her head, surprised by the honesty in her voice. He found it oddly brave of her to admit. Most people would bluster and joke their way through something like this. Not that "something like this" was a common event, but still.

He wanted to say something to make her feel better about facing her family but drew a blank. What did he know about sibling conversations? He had one brother and they hadn't spoken in years. He had long since established his role as the disappointment in his family—he was definitely not one to be doling out advice.

So instead, he found himself shamelessly digging for information. "You must really care about this guy to travel halfway around the world to surprise him," he said. He waited for her to respond, even though he didn't want to hear what he knew she would say.

"I do," she said with a sigh that spoke volumes. He mentally kicked himself for bringing it up. He didn't want to hear about this. He wanted to flirt and tease and watch her laugh with abandon—but instead she was staring off into the distance with such a forlorn expression, he couldn't seem to stop himself.

"Have you been together long?" he asked.

She glanced up at him as though surprised to find him there beside her. Rather insulting, actually. He was usually in demand with women, not forgotten while standing by their side. But even Holly's voice sounded dreamy, like she was lost in memory.

"We've been together forever," she said. She sipped her coffee and he caught a hint of a smile on her lips. "We got engaged," she said.

Her words were a swift kick in the gut and Jack was temporarily paralyzed, unable to form words to respond. Holly looked up and laughed at the surprise on his face.

"When we were in kindergarten," she finished.

He let out the breath that had caught in his chest with what he hoped was a normal sounding laugh. "So it was serious."

"Mmm," she mused, a thoughtful look on her face. "It's been a very long engagement."

"So what happened? You grew apart in grade school?"

Her head fell back as she let out a loud, contagious laugh that had other passersby smiling in their direction. "College," she corrected. "I wanted to see the world, meet people, have exciting adventures and Benjamin.... well, he's a homebody."

Somehow Holly made "homebody" sound like a sexy trait. He had a fleeting and bizarre desire to be a homebody, which was ridiculous.

"But we stayed great friends," she continued. "Best friends."

She stopped talking abruptly so he filled in the blanks. "But now you want more."

He thought she wouldn't respond, she was staring fixedly at the river which had come into view. "Yes," she finally said.

They walked in silence for a bit, sipping their coffee and taking in the view of longboats floating down the Seine. He meant to let it go. He didn't want to hear anymore. But despite himself, he heard his voice asking, "What changed?"

She turned to him with a quizzical look, her forehead creased in confusion. "What?"

"What changed?" he repeated. "What happened to make you want more after so many years as best friends?" He heard the mockery in his tone at the way he said "best friends" and clamped his mouth shut. He sounded like a jealous ex.

She gave a little shrug which he knew to be a lie, although he didn't know how he knew that. He also noticed that she avoided outright answering the question. "I think—when we were younger, he was always cleaning up my messes, you know? He was always getting me out of some scrape or making an excuse to get me out of trouble." She shot him a lopsided grin that rendered him speechless. "I was always in trouble," she added.

"So Mr. Homebody was your knight in shining armor," he said.

She nodded with a twinkling laugh and Jack decided right then and there that he absolutely despised Benjamin, whether it made sense or not.

"That's exactly it," she agreed. "He was my knight."

They came to a stop by the water's edge and Holly gave a little sigh that tore at his heart. "And now I need to convince him that he can trust me. That I won't make a mess of this."

"Make a mess of what?"

She continued as if he didn't speak. "I don't think he trusts me…to be a mom. To make a lifetime commitment."

His heart hurt at the pain he heard in her voice. He'd never met anyone who was so open, so defenseless with their emotions. Her words slowly made their way to his brain and he swallowed down the knee-jerk reaction to run in the opposite direction.

It's not like she was asking *him* to be a husband or father. But still. His feet were ready to run. He had learned a long time ago that he was not that sort of man—the kind people can depend on. Anyone who leaned on him ended up crashing to the ground when he let them down—and he always let them down. Disappointing people, hurting the ones he loved—whether it was intentional or not—that was all he could be counted on to do.

"I get it," he said, shoving his hands into his pockets.

She turned to him in surprise and he instantly knew that she'd misunderstood. "I mean, I understand what it feels like to let people down. To not be trusted by the people you love."

He shifted uncomfortably under her scrutinizing gaze. He didn't regret saying what he'd said—he wanted her to know that he understood what she was going through, at least to a certain extent. But still, he'd never opened up to anyone like that and the fact that she was now staring at him in that all-seeing omniscient sort of way was terrifying.

Forcing a grin, he added. "So yeah, I get the trust part. The kids and family part? Not so much."

Holly laughed at that and rolled her eyes. "Believe me, I know."

His brows shot up at that and it was his turn to study her. She turned away quickly and he was more than a little amused to see a pink blush spreading across her cheeks.

"You know?" he said.

She shrugged and toyed with the lid of her coffee cup. "Yeah, I mean, everybody knows that."

Her vague answer only made him more curious. He was well aware of the reputation he'd made for himself but Holly's unease made him want to know what exactly she thought she knew about him. "Everybody knows what?" he pressed. He couldn't help it, he was absurdly entertained by the sight of her discomfort.

She cast him a look out of the corner of her eye. Turning to face him, she let out an exasperated sigh. "I read the article *Vanity Fair* did on you, okay? You made it very clear that you have no interest in marrying or settling down."

Had he said that? He had a vague memory of that article coming out a couple of years ago but clearly it left an impression on Holly. Jack couldn't stop the smug grin that spread across his face.

"So you've been reading up on me, huh?" he teased.

Holly's lips twitched but she ignored the comment. "Even if I hadn't read that article, you've made it abundantly clear that you are not a one-woman man by your actions." She rolled her eyes as she said, "I don't think I've ever seen you with the same woman twice."

Jack shrugged, ignoring the odd impulse to point out that he'd been spotted with her a number of times now, if anyone was watching. Before he could say anything, she quickly added, "Not that I'm judging. I'm not. I used to be the same way. I had the attention span of a gnat, especially when it came to relationships. But now…" her voice trailed off with another sigh.

"But now you want the whole fantasy—the babies, the minivan, the yard with a white picket fence," he finished for her.

She smacked his arm at his teasing tone but she was smiling. "I know it sounds ridiculous to you. I take it you haven't changed your mind since that article came out—"

He cut her off with an exaggerated shudder. "A wife and kids? Me? Definitely not. Out of the question."

Jack thought she would laugh at that but she looked oddly serious. "That's what I thought."

The silence that followed seemed too heavy and Jack was quick to fill the void. "And that's what you want?" he asked. "A family?"

Her sigh was so wistful, he thought she might cry. "More than anything."

He tugged her arm a bit so she turned toward him. He would do absolutely anything to rid her face of that sad smile. He wanted to tell her that she wasn't a mess—that she was perfect—but he knew she would laugh him off.

He would just have to prove it to her. How? He had no idea.

"Why don't we stay here for a few days?" he said.

Holly's eyes lit up a bit but then her eyes narrowed with wariness. "Are you sure?"

"I'm positive. Danny and Brunelli have been on my case to visit the Paris office so why not now?"

Plus, it would give her time to figure out what to say to her family and him time to convince her that Benjamin was all wrong for her. Not that Jack was the right guy. Obviously. But still, Ivy didn't like this guy and it was the least he could do for his best friend's sister.

She was beaming up at him and for a second, *he* felt like a knight in shining armor. "Thank you," she said.

He gave a shrug and hoped she couldn't see his ridiculously giddy grin. "Don't mention it."

Turning so they were once again heading along the river, he put a hand on her lower back and gently nudged her to continue their walk. "So, where to today?" he asked.

She looked up with wide eyes. "Don't you have to go to the office?"

"It's Sunday," he pointed out.

Her lips twitched up in a self-deprecating grin. "Oh, right." She took his arm again as she led them further down the Seine. "In that case, we should probably start with the Musée D'Orsay, it's my favorite."

* * * *

One museum and two croissants later, they hopped in a cab back to the flat, pleasantly exhausted and desperately in need of a shower. Or at least Holly was. Jack was annoyingly hot with his mussed hair and sunglasses. She on the other hand was a total mess with no makeup and the ratty old T-shirt she'd slept in the night before.

Jack must have been cringing at the sight of her all morning. Not that it mattered. She wasn't here to impress Jack. She was here to come up with a game plan for winning over Benjamin. What better place to come up with a strategy for love than Paris?

They showered and relaxed around the apartment for a bit but Holly was eager to get back out into the city of love. She needed inspiration before she got up the nerve to call Benjamin to tell him where she was… and why.

"You ready yet?" Holly asked, poking her head into the living room where Jack was furiously typing away on his laptop. He glanced up and blinked rapidly as if coming out of a daze. "Oh, yeah. Just wrapping up some work. Give me two minutes." He turned back to the screen and was once more hypnotized.

Holly watched him work for a minute. He was awfully cute when he was working.

But then, Jack was awfully cute all the time. That's why she and half the women in America swooned over his pictures in gossip magazines.

Her cheeks burned all over again at the memory of her big mouth that afternoon. He'd probably thought she was some kind of crazy groupie. She'd all but quoted that article *Vanity Fair* had run on him years ago.... more embarrassing than that, she actually *could* quote parts of that article word for word, she'd read it so many times. She had been royally smitten with the sexy tech genius from the moment he'd begun gracing the tabloids. She'd read all the articles about his romantic exploits—articles which, for a time, featured her sister. Holly grinned as she watched him work. It was hard to believe that she had ever fallen for that story. Or that anyone had, for that matter. Just being in the same room as Ivy and Daniel, it was insanely obvious that they were in love.

To think, she had actually been jealous of her sister for a little while there. Not that she wanted Jack, of course. Her days of dating playboys were long gone. She was ready for the real deal. But still. Holly had a feeling she would be jealous of any woman who managed to tame the sexy playboy.

Could it be done? She thought back to the slew of photos and articles she'd read on him. Highly doubtful. Besides, there could only be one wild child per couple, everyone knew that. Not that she was thinking about trying. Because she wasn't. She'd chosen her partner and he was perfect for her in every way.

Her smile faltered a bit when she thought of Benjamin. Or rather, how Benjamin would react to the news that she was in France. With Jack. He'd said he was fine with the pictures that the Oakdale Gazette had printed, and he *had* seemed to be fine with it. He was very rational like that. But it was just a matter of time before his sisters or mother showed him the *People* magazine picture and there's no way he could be so nonchalant about that.

It wasn't like she had set out to make him jealous but if it *worked*.... maybe this trip to the wrong Paris wasn't such a disaster after all.

Jack hopped to his feet with a wide grin that made her smile in return. "You ready?"

"As I'll ever be," she said. She snatched up a lightweight sweater she'd strewn onto the couch, grabbed her purse and led the way to the door.

"Where to first, my little sightseer?" he asked.

She spun around in the doorway and he nearly collided into her. God, he smelled great. Was that cologne or his soap? The debate was still on. Whatever it was, he should buy it and sell it. With his face on the front, obviously. It would be a hit.

Jack was watching her expectantly, waiting for her answer. Oh right. He'd asked her something. "Lunch," she said. "I'm starving."

He threw a hand over his heart and groaned. "You are a woman after my own heart."

"You're hungry, too?" she asked.

"Always."

The brasserie was dimly lit and smelled amazing. It was crowded but Holly spotted a table in the back. "You go snag us a seat, I'll tell the waitress we're here," Jack said. He lightly gripped her arm as he spoke and he leaned in so his mouth was next to her ear, sending shivers down her spine.

She nodded and headed toward the back. When she took her seat, she glanced up to see if Jack was behind her but instead she found him ensnared. That was the only word for it. A stunningly beautiful woman had her arms around him and was whispering in his ear, a charming smile on her annoyingly perfect face.

Holly sucked in a deep breath to squelch the instantaneous revulsion at the sight before her. She was not jealous, she told herself. That would be stupid. She was just…protective.

And Jack looked miserable, she realized with more than a little delight. He was standing at attention as though suddenly recruited to the army, and his usual charming grin was replaced by a forced, polite smile that screamed, "Help me."

Holly scrambled to get out of the booth. After all, she'd made a promise to return the favor. If there was any doubt in her mind that this woman was one of the many spurned lovers he'd mentioned, it was erased by the possessive way the woman let her hand linger on his arm and the way she leaned in to whisper in his ear.

A surge of adrenaline had Holly practically running across the crowded restaurant. She didn't stop to think, she just acted. After all, she'd made a promise.

"Sweetheart, what's taking you so long?" she said as she cozied up beside Jack, slipping an arm around his waist and wiggling under his arm so it was wrapped around her shoulder. As the woman watched, she leaned in so close her lips were touching his ear. "Now we're even," she whispered.

Jack looked down at her with eyes wide with shock and his mouth open as though to speak but no words immediately came out so she continued to avoid an awkward silence.

She turned a huge smile to the woman before her whose look of surprise matched Jack's. The supermodel recovered quickly and held out a perfectly manicured hand and said in a thick, French accent, "How do you do, I'm Miranda."

"Holly," she responded quickly, shaking the other woman's hand with a bit more force than necessary.

Miranda looked from Holly to Jack and then back again. Holly could see the confusion on her face. Still wasn't clear? Perhaps she should spell it out.

"I'm Jack's girlfriend," she said.

She heard a strangling noise come from Jack and looked up to see him alternating between shock, amusement and...horror. *Uh oh.*

Miranda crossed her arms and took a step back to survey the happy couple. "Is that right?"

Holly was sure the other woman would twirl around on her expensive high heels and storm out, but to her amazement, the woman grinned at them both in sheer joy. "How wonderful!"

Holly looked up to Jack and gave him a questioning look.

Jack cleared his throat. "Holly...honey...allow me to properly introduce you to Miranda *Everett*, my sister-in-law."

Holly's stomach took a nosedive and her heart rate kicked up a notch. *Oh crap.* She looked up at Jack, trying to gauge his reaction. His mouth was twitching but it was impossible to tell if he was smothering a laugh or a curse. Maybe it wasn't too late to clear the air. She looked to the woman across from her and gave her best smile.

"I, uh, I should probably explain. You see, Jack and I aren't—"

"No need to explain, my dear." Miranda was smiling at her with such joy that Holly swallowed the rest of her explanation. "I'm so glad to see that Jack is happy again."

Holly gave Jack a quick sidelong glance, hoping to get some signal as to how she should proceed. But he was useless. He still looked shell-shocked.

To Holly's surprise, Miranda reached out and grabbed her hand, giving it a little squeeze. "You two must come to our apartment tonight. We're hosting a party—something small, just a little gathering of close friends. Please tell me you'll come."

Again Holly glanced up at Jack but he was no help. He had clamped his mouth shut and his lips were thinned into a tight line. He looked unusually...un-charming.

"Well, um, I'm not sure," Holly stammered. Now she was looking at Jack with wide, panicked eyes, trying to telepathically beg him for some assistance. It wasn't working.

"Oh, please," Miranda pleaded. Now she reached out another hand so she was holding both Jack's and Holly's hands in hers and they looked like they were about to burst in "Kumbaya" in the middle of the busy brasserie.

Apparently getting the same lack of reaction from Jack, she turned her attention to Holly. "Please, do come. It would mean the world to Jack's brother."

The gorgeous woman's big brown eyes were pitifully pleading and Holly crumbled. "Of course, we'd love to go."

The woman let out an exclamation of joy before kissing both her cheeks and then Jack's before hurrying out of the restaurant, leaving Holly and Jack standing there alone in a crowd in heavy silence.

When she finally hedged a look at Jack, she found him staring down at her with a grim look but he remained frighteningly silent.

"So," she said with a forced cheeriness. She was at a loss as to how to finish that sentence. *So, I just declared myself your girlfriend to your family. So, you were incredibly awkward around that woman. So, we're going to a party—why do you look like it's your funeral?*

When she didn't finish speaking, he cocked an eyebrow. "So," he repeated. Somehow his "so" sounded far less pleasant.

"So…that happened," she ended lamely.

He turned away from her with an exasperated groan and led the way back to their table, where he slumped into a chair with a defeated air. Holly was more than a little alarmed to see Jack—cheerful, devil-may-care, Jack—wearing a worried scowl.

"I'm sorry," Holly said, sliding into the booth across from him.

To her relief, Jack gave her a wry smile. "It's okay, you were just trying to help."

"So that was your sister-in-law, huh?" she said. "She's awfully pretty."

Jack rolled his eyes. "That's an understatement."

"And she seemed nice," Holly continued, shamelessly digging for information.

"Mmm," Jack agreed. He had turned his attention to the menu a waitress had left on their table.

"So why were you such a weirdo?"

Okay, perhaps that was not the most diplomatic question she'd ever posed but still, she wasn't sure she deserved the gaping look of horror he was sending her way.

"I was not a *weirdo*," he sputtered.

Holly raised a brow in disbelief. "Uh, yeah, you kinda were."

He snapped his mouth shut and made a show of reading the menu. Now it was her turn to stare in disbelief. He was ignoring her? "What are you doing?" she snapped.

He didn't look up. "Reading the menu, what does it look like I'm doing?"

"Moping."

He looked up at that and for a moment, Holly barely recognized him. She was so used to seeing the easygoing, laid-back charmer, this serious man across from her looked like a stranger. His guarded demeanor shattered her defensive anger.

"What happened back there?" she asked, her tone far less accusatory.

Jack tossed the menu down with a sigh and leaned back in his booth. "That's the first time I've seen Miranda since their wedding. That was three years ago."

Holly found herself holding her breath, waiting for him to continue. When he didn't, she asked quietly, "Is that the last time you saw your brother, too?"

Jack gave a quick nod. His jaw was clenched so tight she thought he might chip a tooth.

"What happened?"

For a second she thought he was going to ignore her but after a moment of silence he let out a humorless laugh. "What always happens," he said. "Someone trusts me and then they live to regret it."

Holly's heart ached at the bitterness in his voice. "I'm sure that's not true," she murmured. Even as she spoke the words, she knew how useless they were. She knew better than anyone what it felt like to let down the people around you, to be the flaky unreliable mess that had to be cleaned up after.

She studied him for a moment in silence. Her heart was aching at the sadness she saw there but if there was one thing she knew, it was what he did not need right now—pity.

Leaning back in the booth she picked up the discarded menu and focused on reading as she said, "Well, if you're the family failure, I can't wait to meet your brother."

He looked up in surprise. No doubt he'd been expecting her to deny what a mess up he was. One side of his mouth twitched up. It was a bare hint of a smile but it was a start. "Oh yeah?"

"Mmm," she said, reaching for some bread in the basket on their table. "I mean, if the bad seed in your family is a billionaire genius, what on earth are his other siblings like?"

Jack leaned back in the booth, the hint of a cocky grin making her heart do a little flip flop as her breath caught in her throat. "Well there are only two of us, so I guess you'll see for yourself tonight."

Holly's hand froze in mid-air as she reached for the butter. "We're going?"

He picked up a piece of bread and slathered it with some butter before shoving it in his mouth. "Have you ever said no to a party?" he asked with his mouth full.

Holly couldn't help the loud laugh that had the patrons at surrounding tables staring. "No," she said. "I don't believe I have."

He rewarded her with a sexy grin that made his eyes do the squinty thing she loved. "Nether have I."

They ate their bread in silence for a moment, sharing a silly grin. Then Holly leaned over the table. "You do know you're going to have to tell me what happened between you two eventually, right?"

Jack ignored the question, pointing instead to the piece of bread in his hand. "The bread here is *really* good, isn't it?"

Holly rolled her eyes but let the topic drop—for the moment at least. She'd get it out of him eventually.

Chapter 6

Jack toyed with the cuff on his jacket and stared at his reflection in the mirror. He was studiously ignoring the anxious pit in his stomach, as if by refusing to acknowledge it, the knot would dissipate.

It wasn't working. It had been two years since he'd talked to his brother and that had been when his parents had tricked him into calling the house while Robert was there. Had they really thought that a couple of stilted words on the phone were going to dispel the years of bitterness and resentment between them?

He hadn't actually *seen* his brother since the wedding and even that had been a stilted, awkward affair as both brothers made a show of putting aside their feud for the sake of their parents and Miranda.

He'd known Miranda as long as Robert had, since junior high—that's when his father had been stationed in France and the two boys had both fallen for the girl next door.

His hand froze for a moment while straightening his tie. He couldn't believe Miranda, of all people, had actually bought Holly's act. She knew better than anyone that Jack didn't have "girlfriends". He had "friends", many of whom happened to be women but none of whom were ever called "girlfriend."

She'd probably already told Robert. He could practically hear Robert's voice now, asking her what she'd been thinking inviting his useless brother to their swanky party. Jack straightened in front of the mirror and shoved back the hair that had fallen into his face.

He would go and clear up the misconception about Holly. Lord knows he'd learned his lesson on that one, the last thing he needed was word to spread to his parents that he was in a relationship.

Having to tell them that his engagement with Ivy was a lie had been a nightmare. His mother had actually *cried*, and not because he'd lied—that she'd taken in stride—she'd cried because she was so disappointed that it wasn't real. His mother couldn't understand that he could have a complete and fulfilling life without a wife. Despite all the evidence to the contrary—all of the brief flings and short-lived affairs—she refused to believe that he wouldn't settle down one day. Only a mother could still hold out hope that her grown son could miraculously change his ways. He would be the worst son in history if he let her get her hopes up again…and with Ivy's sister, no less.

Tonight he would show his face, play nice with his brother—assuming Robert didn't kick him out first—and make sure Miranda knew the truth about him and Holly. Then they'd leave and he would treat Holly to a night out on the town and he would knock back whiskeys until this latest awful run in with Robert was a blurry memory.

A knock on his door made him glance at the clock. No more procrastinating, it was time to bite the bullet. He opened the door to find Holly looking more beautiful than ever. His mouth froze on the words he'd been about to say. He was speechless.

She was wearing a dark red slip of a dress—tasteful but sexy as hell. Her curls were artfully tousled, like she'd just come from the beach…or somebody's bed. Her makeup was subtle for the most part—except for her lips, which were a siren red that matched the dress.

She looked incredible.

"You're…you look…." Jack cleared his throat. "You look great."

She grinned up at him and gave his jacket lapel a little tug. "You look pretty good yourself." She tilted her head and narrowed her eyes a bit as though reading his expression. "You ready to party like it's 1999?"

His smile felt forced. "Ready as I'll ever be."

* * * *

By the time they pulled up in front of a modest home near the outskirts of the city, Holly was ready to do just about anything if it meant Jack would relax. He was staring out the window in tight-lipped silence that was all the more disturbing because this was Jack. He didn't do silence and no one in the history of the world would ever describe him as grim.

She impulsively reached out to give his hand a squeeze. He looked over in surprise, as though he'd just woken from a trance. He looked down at her hand on his and she quickly pulled her hand back.

"You ready?" she asked.

For a second she thought he wouldn't answer and he made no move to leave the car. "Of all the brasseries in Paris," he muttered.

"Excuse me?"

He looked over at her with a little smile. "Of all the brasseries in Paris, what are the odds that we walked into the same one today?"

She had to laugh at that. "One in a million," she said. She watched him take a deep breath and psych himself up and leaned in a little closer. "That's why it's meant to be."

His eyes widened in surprise. "How so?"

Holly tossed some hair over her shoulder and feigned a confidence she didn't necessarily feel. "You said it yourself, what are the odds? Maybe this is the universe's way of helping you right a wrong."

He cracked a smile that warmed her heart. "Maybe you're right," he said. He inhaled deeply and turned to her with the crooked grin she loved. "Shall we?"

"We shall."

Miranda answered the door and gave them an enthusiastic reception. She drew Jack in for a hug and gave Holly kisses on both cheeks. "Come in, come in, we're so glad you could make it."

Their apartment was spacious and tastefully decorated but it paled in comparison to Brunelli's palatial suite.

"Everyone is in the living room. Come, follow me." She turned and walked deeper into the apartment with Jack and Holly in tow.

They could hear voices coming from the other room and Holly leaned over to whisper, "Tell me about this plan again?"

Jack's voice was low enough that Miranda couldn't hear and it sent tingles down Holly's spine. "We'll come clean about the fact that we're not really a couple, I'll make nice with my brother for a bit and then we'll run away and drink our faces off."

Holly bit her lip to keep from giggling. "Good plan."

Miranda paused in the doorway to the living room, allowing Holly and Jack a chance to catch up. "Everyone, I'd like you to meet Robert's brother, Jack, and his girlfriend, Holly." She turned to them with a beaming grin. "Jack, Holly, this is everyone."

Holly pasted on a smile and was grateful that Jack took her hand in his in solidarity. They faced a group of twenty people, almost all couples, who were smiling at them in welcome. They were standing a step above everyone else in the doorway to the hall and it made her feel like she was standing on a stage with a spotlight pointed right at her.

Miranda leaned over and whispered, "You'll have to excuse our friends, it's not every day they see a celebrity."

One man who bore a striking resemblance to Jack made his way through the crowd. She could feel Jack stiffen as he approached. The other man stuck a hand out to Jack and they shook in a formal, stilted manner. "Robert, good to see you," Jack said.

Jack turned toward her. "This is my...Holly." There was only a brief hesitation and Holly was fairly certain she was the only one who heard the silence where the word "girlfriend" should have gone.

Robert turned to her with a look that was far from welcoming. He didn't even smile, even though Holly's face felt like it might crack from wearing such a huge grin.

"Welcome," he said. His tone was anything but welcoming and Holly's jaw clenched painfully in her effort to maintain the polite smile.

"You have a beautiful home," Holly said. She pressed her lips together to keep in a nervous giggle. She'd sounded exactly like her mom, the self-proclaimed queen of dinner parties. Miranda murmured her thanks but she wasn't paying attention to Holly, she was too busy glancing back and forth between the two men as though waiting for a fight to break out.

"When did you arrive in Paris?" Robert asked. His face wore a slightly pained expression as though making small talk was physically hurting him.

"Yesterday," Jack said before clamping his mouth shut. Holly watched Jack, waiting for him to continue. Surely that's not all he was going to say. She'd listened to this man charm the pants off of a patisserie owner this afternoon using a handful of rusty French and a smattering of Spanish. But here, standing directly in front of his brother, Jack had turned into a mime.

Come on, Holly, you've dined with warring tribesmen in Africa, you can keep a pleasant conversation going among brothers.

"Have you lived here long?" Her voice came out shockingly high pitched—perhaps so high that only dogs could hear her because no humans in the room paid her any mind.

The crowd of people around them had resumed talking and laughing amongst themselves—no one seemed to notice the ice storm that was brewing in their midst.

"So, have you two always been this weird around one another?" Holly blurted out. Well, that did it. Jack, Robert, and Miranda all swiveled to stare at her.

"Pardon?" Miranda said.

Holly ignored her, her eyes were on Jack. She let out a sigh of relief as one side of his mouth began to twitch before breaking into a full-fledged wicked grin. He was back!

She turned to Miranda, "What I mean is, you've known Jack and Robert forever, right? Were they always like...this?" She gestured between the two men, ignoring Robert's look of shock and trying not to be distracted by Jack's smile.

Now Miranda was the one whose lips were twitching and she slapped a hand over her mouth before shaking her head. "No," she said, her voice choked with laughter. "They used to be rather good friends, actually."

Miranda's soft voice with its gorgeous French accent seemed to have a melting effect on Robert. A bit of the tension eased from his shoulders and the harsh glare on his face softened a bit as he considered Holly.

"Holly, was it? How did you and Jack meet?"

Holly's mind went temporarily blank. "Um," she hedged. Miranda raised her eyebrows with a pleasantly expectant look as Robert continued to study her. Holly got the feeling the whole Ivy debacle was probably something of a sore subject in this family, where everything seemed to be a hot button issue. She looked to Jack for help and to her great relief, he seemed to read her mind.

* * * *

Jack was quick to intervene. Neither of them wanted to mention the Ivy connection in a room filled with curious eavesdroppers. All it would take is one misguided word and the tabloids would be all over them.

Besides, he'd promised himself that he would tell them the truth about Holly and clear the air, no point in delaying the inevitable.

He nodded toward the hallway. "Shall we?" he hinted.

Robert gave a grudging nod and led the way to a large, homey kitchen. Jack was struck by a wave of regret, a common feeling every time his brother's name came up. The guilt and sadness were more poignant than ever standing there in the same room, close in distance but so far away they might as well have been staring at one another across a great divide.

If things had been different between them, maybe this kitchen would be a familiar place, a room where he and his brother and sister-in-law cooked together and shared holidays with his parents. But, instead, he was a stranger in a strange land.

There were matching aprons hanging on a rack near the oven. Did his brother cook? He had no idea. There was a heaviness in his chest that he couldn't shake. Holly's hand slipped into his and gave him a little squeeze, bringing him back to the moment.

The foursome had gathered around the kitchen table and were watching him, waiting for him to speak. Oh right, his relationship to Holly.

"Holly is Ivy's sister," he started. He watched Robert's lips thin into a look of disapproval as Miranda's eyes widened in surprise. Good to know at least two people in the world didn't read *People* magazine.

"I'm sure Mom and Dad told you about what happened between me and Ivy," he started.

Robert's cold voice cut in, "Of course they did. They were devastated."

Jack's mouth went dry and he cleared his throat. He'd known they'd been upset when they'd learned the truth, but "devastated" seemed a bit harsh. Was that true? Had he hurt his family…again?

Memories of his and Robert's falling out all those years ago threatened to spill out into the kitchen. Looking at Robert's cold expression, he could remember every accusation, every harsh word. And the overwhelming guilt. The sinking weight he'd been trying to shed for years.

He cleared his throat again, aware of Holly's questioning eyes. He knew without having to talk to her that she wanted to know if she should intervene. He gave a little shake of his head and he watched her clamp her mouth shut. Stifling a completely uncalled-for laugh at the look of disappointment on her face at having to remain quiet, he turned back to his brother and sister-in-law.

"I've apologized to Mom and Dad for that. They understand that it was an…unusual situation."

Robert's mouth was so pinched, it looked like he'd been sucking lemons. "Yes, they said you were 'doing what needed to be done to make EverTech a success.' How noble." He all but sneered the word noble, his voice dripping with disdain.

The ever-present guilt he always felt around his brother niggled at his stomach but for the first time, the guilt was outweighed by anger. His jaw was so tight, he could barely get the words out. "I wouldn't say it was noble, but I was attempting to take responsibilities for my actions and to make—"

"That's a first." Robert's words were a lead weight in the room.

Jack's mouth clamped shut as a hot flush of anger rushed through him. How many times did he have to apologize?

Before he could respond, Miranda stepped between them, her sweet, calm face a reminder of everything his brother had always been—the golden child, the responsible one, the reliable one…the one who got the girl.

"Please," she said quietly. He and his brother shut their mouths but continued to stare daggers at one another.

Miranda turned her sweet, lovely smile to Holly, who was watching everything closely. He saw her white knuckles clenching the island in the middle of the kitchen and had the feeling she was physically holding herself back from intervening on his behalf.

That thought alone made the tension in his body dissipate, his shoulders relaxing slightly. For the first time in a long time, he wasn't facing his brother alone. He had an ally and at this particular moment she looked like a fiery angel with that red, sexy dress and a halo made of untamed curls.

She met his gaze and gave him a lopsided grin that sent a whole new type of tension ricocheting through his body. For one insane moment, he actually considered taking her by the hand and finding an empty bedroom—or hell, just a coat closet—where he could steal another kiss.

He turned back to his brother and sister-in-law to see them studying him. Robert's face was impassive but Miranda wore a silly grin that nearly made him groan aloud. He knew that grin. Miranda, the romantic, thought he and Holly were really in love.

That was it. Time to set the record straight before this lie got out of hand.

He cleared his throat but before he could begin, Robert said, "So you two are a couple then." He leaned back against the counter with his arms crossed as though daring them to wow him with their love story.

Everything was always a challenge with his brother. Jack's spine stiffened and he fought the defensive feeling that his brother stirred up so easily. He would not rise to the bait. Not this time. He had nothing to hide. "Actually," he started. He cleared his throat again, which suddenly felt tight with emotion.

"Oh here we go," Robert said with a weary sigh. His eyes were filled with disdain as he gave Holly a pitying smile. "Let me guess, he doesn't like the word 'couple'. He's probably convinced you that it's better if you keep things casual, am I right?"

Jack watched Holly stiffen, her jaw clenched as she faced his brother head on. He knew without a doubt that she wanted to lash out but was trying her best to remain calm. He wondered if that's how he looked every time he talked to his brother.

He opened his mouth to respond on her behalf but before he could, Holly said in a quiet, controlled voice, "I believe Jack was just about to explain our relationship before you so rudely interrupted."

Bravo! Jack's heart soared watching Holly put his brother in his place. No one ever did that. Nearly everyone, including Jack, had a tendency to cower before Robert's smug righteousness. Even better was watching Robert's mouth clamp shut and Miranda's attempt to smother a laugh at her husband's expense.

Robert recovered quickly and turned to Jack with one eyebrow cocked in sarcastic curiosity. "So tell me, Jack. Have you finally managed to make a commitment for once in your life?"

Jack ignored the comment. He would not be bullied into telling a lie. "As you may have guessed, Holly and I met under rather...*unusual* circumstances." He turned to see Holly giving him a little smile.

"That may be the understatement of the century," she murmured under her breath, making Miranda giggle. Robert was still watching, waiting.

"So it won't come as a surprise when I say that our relationship is a bit unusual as well," he continued. Even to his own ears, he sounded like he was justifying himself and he hated that. Why did he care what Robert thought?

Jack took a deep breath. *Just spit it out.* Robert, meanwhile, was starting to smile. He looked like the cat who ate the canary as he turned to his wife. "I told you. Jack will never commit." Turning toward his wife, he held out his hand. "Pay up."

Jack looked from Holly, whose eyes were wide with shock, back to his brother. Miranda scowled at Robert and slapped his hand away. "Stop it," she hissed.

Robert just laughed. "Fine, you can pay me later."

"You *bet* on this?" Holly's voice came out in a squeak. "You bet on the fact that Jack wouldn't possibly commit to me."

Robert took a step toward Holly and reached out a reassuring hand. "Oh please don't take it personally. This has nothing to do with you. We didn't even know you when we made the bet." Jack was watching Miranda but she refused to meet his eyes. Her cheeks were growing pink under his scrutiny.

"It's just that we know Jack, that's all," Robert continued. "He's never been able to commit to anything—not family, not business, and certainly not women." He was laughing now, seemingly oblivious to the awkward silence that filled the room.

Holly looked to Jack, as though waiting for him to speak. Defend himself, perhaps. But what could he say? Robert was right, as always. He had lived up to his terrible reputation once again.

When Holly spoke, her voice was strong and clear. "It looks like you owe your wife some money because you are dead wrong."

All three of them stared at her in shock. Jack knew it was coming but couldn't bring himself to stop her. Stepping closer to his side so she could link her fingers through his, she said, "We are very much a couple and we are quite happy."

There was a stunned silence before Jack heard his mother's unmistakable voice coming from the doorway. "I'm so glad to hear that, dear. I always knew my son would find someone wonderful and settle down."

Chapter 7

Holly saw Robert and Miranda twirl toward the doorway in surprise and Jack's grip tightened considerably on her hand. Holly's heart kicked into overdrive. This could not be happening…again.

She and Jack spun around to face the owner of the voice—a pretty, petite older woman who was beaming at her and Jack like she'd just won the lottery. An older gentleman who bore a striking resemblance to Jack and Robert stood behind her. He too was grinning and shaking his head in an "oh you crazy kids" kind of way.

"Um, Jack?" she whispered.

Jack turned to her, a blank look on his face. "Holly Sinclair, I'd like you to meet my mom and dad."

Jack's mom, who introduced herself as Claire, rushed toward her and enveloped her in a tight hug. When she pulled back, she was giving her a huge grin. "It's so nice to meet you."

Holly forced a smile to match Claire's. "You too." Before they could talk further it was Jack's dad's turn to pull her into a bear hug. "Let me take a look at the woman who managed to capture my son's heart," he started.

"Dad, don't get carried away," Jack said from behind his father.

"Yeah, we just started dating, really," Holly added. Jack raised a brow at her over his father's shoulder.

"It's true," he added. "Don't go getting too excited." He was looking at his mother who was bouncing on her toes for a better look at her son's new girlfriend.

"What are you doing here?" Jack asked. "I mean, it's great to see you but Robert and Miranda didn't mention that you'd—"

"We're just stopping by on our way back to the base," Jack's father said. "We were supposed to head back today but when Miranda called and said you were in town, we pushed back our flight."

"You should have told us you were coming to Paris," his mother said, swatting his arm lightly.

"Oh well, this trip was really just a last minute impulse," he said. Holly noticed he was actively avoiding looking at her, but whether it was because he was angry or afraid he'd burst out laughing remained to be seen.

His mother looked back and forth between Jack and Holly and sighed. "A weekend getaway to Paris, how romantic."

"Mom, please don't get carried away," Jack said, a note of warning in his voice. Holly remembered what his brother had said about how upset his mother had been when she learned that his relationship with Ivy was a lie and the guilt that had been gnawing at her stomach grew a million times worse.

Holly fidgeted with the strap of her purse, trying desperately to fade into the wallpaper.

The whole point of coming here tonight was to set the record straight and she'd gone and dug the hole even deeper. But really, it wasn't entirely her fault. The way Robert was talking to his brother, demeaning him—she would have done anything to take that smug look on his face. Was it really her fault that she just happened to have the absolute worst timing on the planet?

Once the initial excitement settled down, Holly watched Jack's family interact. With their parents acting as buffer, Jack and Robert were on their best behavior. They never spoke directly to one another but she noticed that they laughed at one another's jokes and listened to each other's stories. If she hadn't seen the tension between the brothers with her own eyes, Holly would have been convinced they were one big happy family.

Holly did her best to stay on the outskirts and not get drawn into their intimate family reunion but neither his parents nor Miranda would allow her keep her distance. After a while she gave up trying and found herself being treated like a long lost member of the family.

When they went to leave a little while later, his mother made them swear that they would meet up again for dinner on their last night in town.

* * * *

Stepping out of the cozy apartment and into the fresh night air, Holly inhaled deeply and let it out with a sigh. "We survived," she said.

"Barely."

She glanced over to see Jack watching her with a wry smile. "Okay, I'll say it," she said. "I'm really sorry I made your parents think we're a couple."

"I'm not." She looked over in surprise at that and he added, "I think we did a fairly good job of clarifying that we're not serious so it won't come as a shock when we break up."

The words gave her heart a bit of a pang but she shook off her own nonsense. Breaking up should not be painful for two people who were not in a relationship.

"Besides, it was nice to see them so happy, even if it's not totally real."

"They did seem pretty happy."

He laughed, "Even Robbie managed to loosen up a bit, did you notice?"

She nodded. "So when are you going to tell me what happened there?"

They were strolling back toward the city center and Jack shoved his hands in his pockets. "Simple, really. We were always competitive. Always. But Robert always won. He got the good grades, kicked my butt in sports, and got the girl."

She peered over at him, her suspicions confirmed. "Miranda, you mean?"

He rolled his eyes. "Don't go getting crazy ideas. I got over that one quickly. It's obvious that she chose the right brother."

"What happened?" she prodded.

"Oh the usual, she was ready for a commitment and I...couldn't give it to her."

Holly ignored the pain in her jaw from clenching it so hard. "So it was serious between you two then."

Jack gave a little nod. "It was serious for a little while. But then she wised up and realized I don't have long-term potential. Not like Robert."

Holly studied his profile. He didn't seem too terribly broken up about his lost love—in fact he sounded a bit bored.

"How long ago was this?"

"High school."

Holly stopped walking and he had to turn to face her.

"High school?" she repeated. "How old were you?"

"Seventeen."

"Seventeen?"

"Why do you keep repeating me?" he asked, that slow smile spreading across his face, making him look entirely too sexy under the soft glow of the streetlamps.

"Because you were *seventeen*," she said. "Of course you weren't ready to make a commitment. You'd just learned how to shave, you couldn't possibly have been ready to make a lifetime commitment."

Jack let out a little laugh and kept walking. "I told you, that's all in the past. She and Robert are a much more logical fit."

"Okay, so then what else?"

Jack sighed again and for a moment she thought he wouldn't respond. But then he said, "That was just the first of many times I let everyone down. Especially Robert. We started growing apart during college, when Robert became even more...."

"Smug? Superior? Self-righteous?" Holly suggested.

"Stubborn. And I became more and more...willful." He ignored her sarcastic snort and continued. "Push came to shove shortly after graduation when I asked Robert to be a backer in my company. He still had some money left from our inheritance from our grandparents. I'd blown through all of mine, of course, but Robert had squirreled his away as a nest egg for him and Miranda."

"And?" Holly nudged. She had an idea where this was going but she wanted to hear the whole story for herself.

Jack shoved his hands into his pocket. "I was supposed to be the idea man—they were my prototypes we wanted to make—and my friend Evan would handle the business end. He'd gotten his degree in business and marketing and he was one of my best friends. I trusted him."

He was silent for a little while and seemed lost in thought. "So, Robert leant you the money..." she prodded.

"And I lost it all. Every penny."

Holly gasped, more from the self-loathing tone in his voice than anything else.

"The worst part was, by the end of it Evan ended up owning all of the intellectual property, so he found other investors and started from scratch with my ideas but without me. Or my brother."

"Oh my God," she murmured. Her heart ached at the bitterness she heard in his tone.

"But that's not your fault," she said.

He glanced over at her with a wry smile. "If only Robbie felt that way."

Before she could protest further, he said, "I may not have been the total traitor that Evan was, but I failed my brother. I promised him that I would see it through, that I would commit to the business. I made him believe that he could trust me to do something right for a change."

Holly placed one hand on his arm. She wished she could do more but even that brief touch seemed far more intimate than it should. He stopped and turned so they were facing one another, only inches between them. Every bit of guilt and resentment was etched on his face and Holly realized that she would do absolutely anything to make his pain go away.

Jack's eyes were filled with self-reproach. "You've got to understand. Our whole childhood and all during high school, I was always getting into trouble and Robbie was always getting me out. Even in college I was always starting projects but never seeing them through. I managed to convince Robbie to trust me for once in his life and he did. And I blew it. I should have been paying attention to the deals Evan was making, I should have read the fine print. I should have been responsible with the money that I was making…but instead I partied it up like a rock star and let Evan take everything."

Holly reached out again and let her hands rest on his shoulders. She waited until his eyes locked with hers before she spoke. "You were young and naïve and you trusted the wrong person. That doesn't make you the bad guy."

The look in his eyes was so soft, so vulnerable, it took Holly's breath away.

"Try telling Robert that," he said. "That was my one chance to prove to my brother that I'd changed—that I wasn't the screw-up kid he's always seen me as…" his voice faded off and he shrugged.

"But you *were* a kid," she said. How did he not see that? How did his brother and the rest of his family not recognize that? Frustration was slowly replacing sympathy and she crossed her arms across her chest and gave him the look that her second graders had dubbed the "stare of doom."

"Listen up, Jack Everett," she said. "You have got to stop blaming yourself for things that happened when you were young and dumb. You are a grown up now so it's time to act like one."

His grin turned to a smirk and she saw the frustration in his eyes when he said, "So what are you saying, I should rush out and get married?"

Holly shook her head in annoyance. "Of course not. Marriage doesn't make you responsible. Any idiot can throw a wedding. If you want people to respect you, then you've got to demand respect. Prove that you've changed."

"Is that what you're doing?" His quiet words stopped her tirade and for a moment, her voice caught in her throat.

"Yes," she said. "That's exactly what I'm doing."

His eyes moved over her face, studying her but she had no clue what he was looking for. She wasn't used to feeling like an open book but with Jack sometimes she got the sense that he saw more than she knew—more than she wanted anyone to see.

A small smile eased the taut silence. "And how's that working out for you?"

Maggie Dallen

She felt her lips twitching up against her will. She was such a coward. "I'll let you know once I talk to Benjamin."

She could have sworn she caught him flinch when she said Benjamin's name. *Interesting.* Before she could give it any more thought, he'd resumed walking so she had to do a little skip in her high heels to catch up.

"I believe it was agreed we would follow up tonight's familiar fun by drinking our faces off, correct?"

Holly reached his side and linked her arm through his. "Let's do this."

* * * *

Holly really shouldn't make important phone calls after she'd had several cocktails. It wasn't rocket science. She should know better. But she called him anyway.

By the time they stumbled into the apartment a couple hours later, laughing their heads off, Holly had an overwhelming need to call Benjamin. The drinks had done their job and ebbed away any humiliation she might have felt at having to explain that she'd tried to chase after him…and failed. It was time to finally come clean about her feelings. He should just be finishing up with his training for the day. The timing was perfect. Holly headed straight for her bedroom when they got inside.

"You going to bed already?" Jack slurred. He'd had far more drinks than she'd had. But then he was the one recovering from a rather dramatic family reunion. She'd just been there to help.

She threw him a smile over her shoulder as she kicked off her heels in the hallway. "Got a phone call to make," she said.

"Ah," she heard him say behind her. "Good luck!"

She didn't need luck. Benjamin knew her better than anyone. Once he found out that she'd followed him halfway around the world, he would get it. He would understand why she'd done what she did. There would be no more dancing around the issue—no more playing coy. Closing the bedroom door behind her she got out her phone and plopped down on the bed. This was it. Time to fess up. She took a deep breath. He would understand and everything would be fine. Things were always fine with Benjamin. She exhaled on a sigh and slowly pecked out the numbers on her long distance phone card.

He picked up on the first ring. "Please tell me my mom is wrong," he said in lieu of a hello.

"Your mom is wrong," she said on autopilot. But her stomach was slowly sinking. This was not the warm, welcoming hello she'd been hoping for. This conversation was not off to the greatest start.

"Please tell me you're not really in Paris, France," he said, his voice laced with impatience.

The fact that he knew where she was without being told didn't surprise her. She should have known he'd have heard by now. The Oakdale gossip machine was more efficient than the Associated Press in spreading news. She was positive Ivy had told her mom, who'd told his mom, who'd told him. She rarely had to break any news to Benjamin herself. He was always two steps ahead whenever there was a crisis. Not that being in Paris, France, counted as a *crisis*, per se. Her mind flashed on a particularly fun club they'd gone to, with an outdoor patio and a killer jazz band.

"Earth to Holiday," Benjamin said. The use of her nickname brought her crashing back to the present and she leaned back against the headboard, giving her tired, aching feet a much needed rest.

"Don't panic, Benjamin, I'm fine," she said, using her best soothing tone—the one she'd used to comfort him when he'd freaked out that she'd caught malaria—as if it was somehow her fault a mosquito had bit her.

"My mom said you were in Paris...France," he said. The warm fuzzy feeling brought on by the cocktails was fading fast. He actually sounded...annoyed.

"Ummm."

"Holiday," her nickname came out on a long suffering sigh and Holly threw her hands up in exasperation.

"What? It was an accident. I'm sure I'm not the first person to go to the wrong Paris."

Was she? She'd never considered it. Maybe she *was* the first.

His silence was deafening. She could practically see him frowning on the other end, his oh-so-practical brain trying to make sense of her not-so-practical actions. She needed to get this conversation back on track. This wasn't about where she was, it was about why she was there.

"Benj, it's really not that big of a deal. I needed to fly to Europe soon anyway, I'm just here a little—"

"Why did you go to Paris?" his voice cut her off. She had expected confusion, even some exasperation, perhaps. But she hadn't expected him to be so...cold.

"I wanted to surprise you," she said.

"Why?"

Tears appeared almost instantaneously at the sharp tone in his voice. She swiped them away with her hand and sat up in bed. "I was trying to be romantic," she said. The words came out before she thought them through and she instantly wished she could take them back.

This wasn't right. That wasn't how she'd intended to tell him. Not like this. Not when he was angry with her and she was half a world away.

She waited for him to say something—anything. She'd just admitted that she had feelings for him and he was silent. This was not the sweet, loving conversation she'd imagined they'd be having. Seconds ticked by as she waited for him to speak. The fact that she couldn't see his expression was killing her. *Say something*, she wanted to shout. But she didn't. The lump in her throat kept her silent.

"Where are you staying?"

Holly cleared her throat. "Brunelli's apartment in the city."

"Alone?" He sounded so distant, his voice unreadable. She tried to form the words "With Jack," but they wouldn't come out.

At her silence, he sighed again and she had the horrible feeling she'd disappointed him. She found herself kicking her legs against the side of the bed like a sulking teenager. This was not how the conversation was supposed to go.

"You're with Jack, aren't you?" he asked. "Ivy told your mom he was coming to get you."

Coming to get you. Why did everyone seem to think she was a helpless victim in need of saving? No, not everyone. Just Benjamin and her family. "Yeah, he's here too," she said.

"I saw the picture." There was not even a hint of jealousy in his tone. He was just stating a fact.

"What picture?"

"Don't play dumb," he said with a short laugh.

The lump in her throat made talking difficult. "Nothing happened. I told you it was just a kiss."

"It doesn't matter."

Her head jerked back as if she'd been slapped across the face. No words could have hurt more at that moment. Why didn't it matter? Why didn't he care?

"He's not good for you, Holiday." There it was, the overprotective big brotherly tone she knew so well. At that moment she despised that tone.

"Then who is?" The words slipped out and the urgency in her own voice took her by surprise.

I am. She willed him to say it but all she got was stony silence.

Then he sighed. "What do you want me to say, Holiday?"

Holly's breath caught as her heart moved to her throat. "I want—" she started. "I want you to give us a shot." There was another long, heavy silence before she added, "As a couple."

Her heart was out there, hovering in the silence as she waited for him to speak. And the silence was almost answer enough. This couldn't come as a complete surprise, not after all the flirting, the hints, the innuendos. She'd all but spelled out her feelings from the first day she arrived back in Oakdale.

"I'm just not sure it's what's best for you."

Holly's body went numb and she pressed her lips together to stifle a sob. It wasn't the words that stung so much as the tone. She knew him well enough to know when he was being honest and right now—it was killing him to tell her the truth. He was trying to be nice— he was trying to save her. She'd thought his constant concern for her had meant he cared about her as more than just a friend. And now…maybe she'd been wrong all along.

She took a deep breath but a wave of anger and hurt washed over her making her tremble. "Stop worrying about me for once. I don't need you to save me from myself."

All she got was a shocked silence. Benjamin had never been one for confrontations. He preferred to give people space. Well too bad. She'd been waiting to have this conversation for too long. She'd been tiptoeing around the topic out of respect for his delicate sensibilities when it came to hashing things out. She was done waiting.

"Don't make this about me. I know what I want. What about you? Is it what you want?"

When he didn't answer, she gripped the phone tighter and tried to swallow back the bile that was rising in her throat. "Benjamin, do you want to be with me?"

A heavy silence fell between them before Benjamin exhaled loudly. "No, I don't think so."

Holly felt like she'd been punched in the gut as the wind rushed out of her lungs. She heard him say her name but her throat closed up, making a response impossible, even if she knew what to say.

* * * *

Jack should have gone to bed. He'd had one drink too many and would be paying for it in the morning. If he was smart, he would pop some aspirin, drink a couple glasses of water, and shut his brain off with some much needed sleep.

Instead he found himself sprawled out across one of the deck chairs on the patio, staring up at the cloudy sky. It looked bright, thanks to the reflection of city lights. But what he saw was Holly. An image of her, laughing over one of his stupid jokes, her head thrown back revealing a long, slim neck. Her face scrunched up in a grin and her eyes…her eyes were magic. In that bright red dress she'd looked way too good for the dive bar they'd found themselves in after Robert's disastrous party.

He tried to shove thoughts of Robert to the side. Images of Holly might be torturous but they were delicious. His brother? Not so much.

If you want people to respect you, then you've got to demand respect. Prove that you've changed. Holly's voice taunted him. Rubbing a hand over his face, he cursed out loud. What did everyone think he'd been doing these past few years? He'd been working his butt off to make EverTech a success, he'd paid his brother back every dime he'd lost with interest and he'd become a world famous success story. But all his brother saw was the playboy in the gossip rags, the unreliable kid who'd made a mess of his life.

And it was his fault. That's the image he presented to the world and everyone, including his family, believed it.

And rightfully so. He shook his head and struggled upright into a sitting position. Who was he trying to kid? Look at the mess he'd gotten himself into with Holly tonight, letting his family believe he was actually in a *relationship*, God forbid. And the ludicrous mishap he'd started with Ivy and Daniel because of one stupid stunt? He hadn't changed. Despite the new success financially, he was still the same screw up he'd always been.

Robert saw what his friends and Holly refused to believe. *You can fool your friends but you can't fool family.*

He rested his elbows on his knees and allowed his head to drop into his hands. It was the same old story with him. He did one silly, reckless thing and suddenly he ruined the lives of everyone around him. He'd thoughtlessly kissed Miranda when they were young, not giving one thought to the fact that his brother had been pining for her for years. He'd signed on the dotted line with his best friend without a second glance. He'd dropped on one knee in a stupid gesture and turned Ivy's world upside down. He'd crushed his parents' dreams time and time again by flitting from one woman to the next, from one party to the next, from one country to the next. It was who he was. A screw-up.

Was it any wonder Holly was looking for a man who was the exact opposite from the sounds of it?

And there it was. Right back where he'd started. All thoughts led to Holly.

What was she doing now? Probably sleeping like any sane person would. It was the middle of the night and they'd been out partying for hours. Of course she was asleep.

Images of Holly in bed flooded his brain. Her curls strewn across his pillow, a naked thigh tossed over his. He sucked in a deep breath of fresh air. *Do not go there.*

Holly was asleep, most likely dreaming of her perfect soon-to-be boyfriend. *Benjamin.* Jack thought the name in a taunting sing-song voice. He had officially devolved into a child thanks to his ridiculous infatuation with his new roommate and pretend girlfriend.

Jack hoisted himself off of the chaise lounge with a groan. It was official; he was going to be in a world of pain come morning. Shuffling into the kitchen to grab a glass of water to wash down his aspirin, he stopped short at a sound coming from the living room.

He thought he was hearing things since the lights were off, but no, there was definitely sound coming from the dark room. Heading to the living room doorway, he poked his head inside.

There she was. The woman he'd been fantasizing about for the last hour was curled up in a ball on the couch, with an old black-and-white film flickering in the background, the volume on low. From where he stood, Jack could only see the top of her head and her feet, which were sticking out from beneath a blanket.

He tip-toed toward her, thinking he would shut off the TV and wake her so she could go sleep in a proper bed. But as he drew close, he heard it. She was sniffling. Jack froze, his senses on high alert. Then he heard a little hiccup.

His stomach sank. *Oh God. She was crying.*

She must have heard him approach because she sat up a bit to peer over at him. Jack's heart tightened painfully. Even in the dim glow from the TV screen he could make out the tears that were trickling down her cheeks.

Moving to her side, he wedged himself into the space where her head had been, forcing her to lie against him as he wrapped his arms around her. She stiffened for a moment before relaxing against him with a heavy sigh. He refused to acknowledge how amazing it felt to have her pressed against him. She fit perfectly, like she'd been made to lie in his arms.

He ran one hand over her back in what he hoped was a soothing gesture as the other held her tight against his chest. Her curls tickled his nose as she buried her face in his chest. He focused on the vanilla scent of her perfume to keep his mind from obsessing over the feel of her in his arms. Now was not the time—he was being chivalrous, dammit.

He felt her breathing slow a bit and soon her shoulders stopped shaking. For a moment he thought she'd fallen asleep laying half on top of him.

Not that he would have minded. Jack would have been happy to stay like that all night if it meant she wasn't crying anymore.

But she eventually stirred and pushed herself away from him, using his chest as leverage. Her face was so close to his, he could feel her warm breath against his cheek. His skin burned beneath her hands and the tightness in his chest spread to his groin. He should move away from her. She no longer needed to be held and he didn't have the willpower to keep from crushing her against him. He should go.

Despite his absolute conviction that he should move far away from temptation, his body remained glued to her side. It seemed to have a mind of its own.

He brushed an errant curl out of her face and let his fingers graze her cheek, wiping away the remnants of her tears. "What happened?" he asked.

The sadness that still lingered in her eyes was unbearable to see. He watched her take a deep, shaky breath. "H-he doesn't want me."

The hand that had been idly playing with one of her curls stilled. Ice washed through his veins and his mind went blank with incomprehension. The fact that any man didn't want this woman was incomprehensible. And the fact that she was so heartbroken over any man who could be so idiotic and blind was unbelievable.

He fumbled for something to say. "Benjamin?"

She nodded. *Of course, Benjamin. Who else?* His stomach turned in disgust and he fought the rage that threatened to take over. He took a deep, steadying breath. This was not about him or that jackass Benjamin. Holly was in pain and that was all that mattered.

The last thing Jack wanted was to hear about her infatuation for this idiot but he forced himself to say, "Do you want to talk about it?"

Holly's lower lip trembled and Jack was sure he'd never seen anything more heartbreaking than Holly's struggle to refrain from crying. Then the words spilled out of her, so fast at first he could barely keep up.

It was a struggle to keep his rage in check. He focused on maintaining what he hoped was a sympathetic look on his face as his fists clenched and unclenched against the sofa cushions.

When she finally finished by telling him Benjamin's parting words that apparently had been the death blow to Holly's dreams, he couldn't take it anymore. He moved so he could face her and gripped her shoulders so she was forced to look into his eyes.

Some of his anger must have been clear because her eyes widened in surprise. "I need you to listen to me," he said. She gave a little nod. His eyes locked with hers as he said slowly, "Benjamin is an idiot."

There was a brief silence as Holly stared back at him and then he saw the tiniest hint of a smile touch her lips.

He thought his heart might explode. That little flicker of a smile made him feel like Superman. "I'm serious, Holly. This Benjamin guy may be the biggest loser on the face of the planet if he can't see how amazing you are."

The tiny smile grew a bit and she let out a little laugh and rolled her eyes. "Well, now you're just being nice."

He leaned back a bit and pretended to be horrified. "I would *never*."

She giggled a bit and the ice in his veins vanished, only to be replaced by a liquid heat that was entirely inappropriate.

His eyes locked with hers as he continued. "I'm serious. You are the most amazing woman I've ever met. You're gorgeous, obviously, but you're also down to earth and funny and you have a lust for life that is awe inspiring."

He watched her expression shift from amused to touched, her eyes softening as she leaned in closer. He shifted so he could wrap an arm around her. She fit so perfectly against his side, it felt like a puzzle piece clicked into place as she snuggled up against him.

Tilting her head back, she was once again looking into his eyes.

"I'm serious, you know," he said.

Her voice was little more than a whisper. "Thank you."

"He's a fool," he said, his voice had lowered, too. Time seemed to slow down as their gazes locked. Her lips were so tantalizingly close, it was unbearable. His already fuzzy brain was having a hard time piecing words together, it could only focus on the feel of her body pressed against his and the heat that coursed through him, begging to be released.

She leaned in closer. "I don't want to talk anymore."

Chapter 8

She was a fool. This was wrong, so wrong. But it felt so *right*.

She watched Jack's eyes cloud over with desire but he held himself away from her, his body rigid beneath her hands.

She leaned in closer.

"We shouldn't," he said, his voice so low she almost couldn't hear him.

She nodded. "You're right, we shouldn't. But I want to."

Closing the distance she lightly brushed her lips against his. It was a brief, almost chaste kiss but it was enough to make all of the blood in her body rush with desire and her heart rate doubled.

For a moment she thought he wouldn't respond. She went to pull back but then his stiff composure crumbled and he snaked a hand through her curls, crushing his lips against hers with an urgency that was undeniable.

His arm around her tightened so she was pressed firmly against him. But still it wasn't enough. She wanted to get closer, to lose herself in this intoxicating kiss. He groaned when she wrapped her arms around his neck. In one quick movement, he pulled her so she was sprawled across his lap. He moved his lips over hers, deepening the kiss.

Holly was melting. Every horrible emotion she'd been battling since that phone call was washed away by pure, unbridled desire. Her skin was burning up and there was an ache between her thighs that bordered on painful. She pressed her breasts against his chest and let her hands run over his neck and shoulders, holding him to her. She was holding on for dear life.

His tongue tangled with hers, stroking her mouth and leaving her breathless. She moaned in ecstasy and her head dropped back as she gasped for air. His head dipped to trail kisses down her neck until she was panting for air.

Her fingers tugged at the hem of his T-shirt, until she inched it up enough for her hands to slip underneath. She was desperate to feel his warm skin and his hard chest beneath her fingertips.

His hands had moved from her back to her sides and when one hand slid up to cup her breast, which was bare beneath the nightshirt, she nearly lost it.

"Please," she said, the word coming out on a moan as he found her hard nipple beneath the thin fabric.

He froze at the sound of her voice. His hands stilled against her and she could feel his muscles grow taut beneath her hands. Oh no, no, no. He couldn't stop now. She wanted this more than she'd ever wanted anything. She needed him.

Holly drew back so she could see his face. Her stomach plummeted as the aching throb at her core intensified. He was going to pull away.

"We can't," he said. "We shouldn't."

She shook her head. She didn't want to hear his rationalizations. He was pulling away from her, rejecting her. That's all she knew.

"No," she said. She heard the anger in her own voice and was surprised by it. Jack's eyes met hers and she held his gaze.

"You don't want this, you don't want—"

"I want *you*," she said. "I want this more than I've ever wanted anything in my life." As the words tumbled out of her mouth she recognized that they were the truth. She couldn't remember ever wanting anything more. For the first time in what felt like forever, she felt like herself. Here in Jack's arms, she was home—she was exactly where she wanted to be.

He paused for a moment and she saw temptation war with responsibility. "I shouldn't. I'd be taking advantage, you're not—"

Holly cut him off again. She shifted so she was straddling his lap, the hard bulge of his erection pressed against the aching heat between her thighs. This time her voice was loud and clear. "Don't tell me what I want or what I'm ready for. I know what I want and I want you. In bed. Right now."

She saw his eyes flicker over her face. Whatever he saw must have convinced him that she knew what she was doing because he scooped her into his arms and lifted her from the sofa, her legs wrapped around his waist.

Pressed against his hard chest, she could feel his heartbeat thundering against her breasts. She buried her face against his neck, letting herself get lost in his masculine scent. She heard his quick intake of air as her lips pressed against his neck, her tongue tasting the skin beneath his ear.

He let out a growl of impatience as he tugged at the hem of her nightshirt and whipped it off of her in one fluid movement. She moaned aloud at the exquisite torture of his hard chest pressed against her breasts.

Her heart was pounding as he set her down on his bed. She wanted this, of that she was sure. A surge of fear passed through her but she fought it. It wasn't fear of this man or what they were about to do—it was how she would feel after. This wasn't just any man—this was the man she'd had a crush on from afar for years. The man who'd swept her off her feet with a simple dance. But more than that…she wouldn't be able to walk away if this ended badly. He had become one of her sister's closest friends over the past year and an inextricable part of her life. It would never just be sex between them.

Things were about to get complicated.

All thoughts and fears were erased when he leaned over her, following her onto the bed. His weight settled against her and they stayed that way for a moment, silent except for their beating hearts and heavy breathing.

He was a dark silhouette against the moonlit room as he hovered over her, giving her every chance to come to her senses.

The last vestige of doubt disappeared. Not just because she wanted this man more than she'd ever wanted anything but because he was waiting for her to say so. She knew he would wait all night or walk away without a word at her say so.

But that's not what she wanted. Thoughts of Benjamin and his rejection threatened to slip back into her consciousness. That was what she wanted to escape. And she could think of no better way to move on than with the most gorgeous man she'd ever seen in her life. There were worse remedies for heartbreak.

"Kiss me," she whispered.

He leaned toward her but still held himself just out of reach. "Are you sure?"

"If you ask me that again, I might slap you," she whispered back.

She saw his grin even in the shadows and it made her heart do a somersault. God, she loved that smile. Then all thoughts were gone as his lips claimed hers and moved over them, gently at first before gentleness gave way to an urgency that was as exhilarating as it was breathtaking.

He ripped off his shirt before lowering his body on top of hers and she couldn't stop her groan of pleasure. He was hard everywhere she was soft and his heat warmed her to the core, replacing the freezing pain that rejection had left behind. Her hands slipped around his body to hold him close, caressing his back and neck as he moved his lips from her mouth to her neck and then up to nibble on her ear. When his tongue flicked out to tease her sensitive earlobe, she gasped and she could feel that smile against her neck.

"My turn," she said, before pushing him so he landed flat on the bed and she was straddling him, naked except for her panties.

She saw his eyes clearly in the glow of the moon and he was staring up at her with such awe and admiration it made her heart ache. "My God, you're beautiful," he whispered.

Leaning down, she let her breasts brush against his chest and his erection pressed against her thighs. He groaned as she moved against him, reveling in the feel of his warm, hard chest brushing against her nipples.

She continued the teasing until he let out a growl and used one hand to pull her head toward him for a deep, thorough kiss. His tongue teased hers as his other hand moved up so he could cup her breasts.

His touches made her weak and she let herself collapse against him. He rolled her over so she was trapped beneath him. She shifted so he was firmly wedged between her thighs, his erection pressing against her. Aching for the feel of him inside of her, she arched against him, urging him to take her.

He reached between them to rid them of their remaining scraps of clothes and pulled her back into his arms. He eased into her as his tongue slipped inside of her mouth, mimicking the long, slow thrust.

She arched her hips to meet him and he lifted his head just far enough that he was looking into her eyes. The moment was intimate and struck a part of her she hadn't known existed. He was looking into the very heart of her. Never before had she been so vulnerable but she couldn't look away. The tension between them built with each thrust until she was on the precipice between desire and aching pain. He claimed her lips then and she climaxed over the edge into ecstasy.

When she came back to her senses, Jack was sprawled on top of her, spent and possibly sleeping. A slow smile of utter contentment spread across her face. She ran her hands over his back, reveling in the solid feel of him and the drowsy pleasure that left her body tingling. She thought she might melt into the mattress she was so pleasantly relaxed.

Jack stirred. He went to move off of her but she tightened her grip around his waist. "Don't go, not yet," she whispered.

He kissed the side of her neck and wrapped his arms around her. "I'm going to crush you," he said with a low chuckle that sent shivers down her neck. He whispered, "How about we do this?" And in one smooth motion, he'd rolled them so he was lying on his back and she was sprawled atop him.

She nestled her head into the crook between his shoulder and chest and let her hands drift across his hard chest. "Mmmm," she said with a sigh of contentment. "Even better."

She could hear his soft laugh through his chest and gave him a little kiss. He stroked her hair with one hand while the other arm wrapped around her, holding her close. That was how she fell into a deep, dreamless sleep.

* * * *

The sound of a slamming door woke her up hours later. She sat up with a start and saw a sleeping, insanely handsome Jack beneath her. The events of the night before clicked into place just as his eyes started to open.

"What's going on?" he muttered. God he was gorgeous when he was sleepy.

"I don't know, I thought I heard—"

"Hello? Anyone home?" a female voice called out.

Holly's wide eyes met Jack's shocked stare. They were frozen in silence for a moment.

"Anyone home?" the voice said again with a distinct Italian accent.

Holly stared at Jack and watched as comprehension dawned in those gorgeous baby blues of his. "Lucia," he whispered. Recognition was quickly replaced with horror. She could have sworn he muttered, "They're going to kill me." Before he shot up out of bed and scrambled to find clothes.

She cursed under her breath. They were in Jack's room and he'd dispensed with her nightshirt somewhere between the living room and the bedroom which meant she had no clothes aside from her panties. Jack was one step ahead of her and he threw her one of his dress shirts. It was long enough to cover her so she could race to her own room.

Holly cracked open the bedroom door and looked back at Jack who was frantically throwing on pants. "Good luck," he mouthed. His roguish grin was almost painfully adorable. She ran over and gave him a little peck on the cheek. "See you on the flip side," she whispered before slipping into the hallway.

She was halfway to her own room and heard Lucia in the kitchen. She could make it…almost there…just a few more feet….

"Ciao, Holly," Lucia's bright voice made Holly jump as she froze mid-tip-toe in the hallway. The petite brunette had come around the corner and was beaming at her. "Surprise!"

Despite the awkward predicament, Holly grinned at her friend who she'd spent so much time with while planning her sister's wedding. The Italian stunner's gregariousness was contagious. "Welcome to Paris," she said with a laugh.

"Sorry I didn't call," Lucia started with a charmingly unapologetic smile. "My grandpa said you two were staying here and I thought you might want some compa—"

Lucia stopped abruptly and her eyes grew wide as her gaze traveled behind Holly. *Uh oh.* Holly glanced over her shoulder and saw Jack stepping out of the bedroom behind her, looking incredibly hot with his bedhead hair and five o'clock shadow. Despite the situation, Holly found herself staring at him in open admiration.

"Hey, Lucia, what a nice surprise," he said. Holly spun back around to see her friend struggling unsuccessfully to keep from laughing. Her knowing eyes flitted from Jack to Holly, who was half-clad in a men's shirt and was clearly coming from the same bedroom that Jack had just exited.

She shot Jack a look over her shoulder. Smooth, real smooth. He shrugged one shoulder as if to say 'the jig is up' and slipped past the two women. "Uh, if you'll excuse me, I think I'll hop in the shower."

"Thanks a lot," Holly muttered as he passed, causing Lucia to lose the battle and burst out laughing.

Jack shot her a mocking grin behind Lucia's back before closing the bathroom door. She turned to Lucia with a shrug. "So..." she started.

Lucia grabbed her arm and started to lead her into the kitchen. "Come with me, I want to hear everything."

* * * *

Lucia had thoughtfully brought croissants and coffees for the houseguests and once they were settled in with breakfast, she fixed her eyes on Holly. "Okay, spill."

Holly hesitated for a moment. She hadn't had a chance to analyze what had happened herself. "I think you can guess what happened," she said, take a big bite of her pastry.

Lucia grinned at her over her cup of coffee. "Yeah, I got that much. But when did this start? And how? And..." Holly watched her friend hesitate. She knew what was coming. "What happened to Benjamin?"

Holly took a deep breath. "He dumped me." She waited for a stab of pain but all she felt was a mild throb of hurt. Maybe she was numb or something. She was sure the full heartbreak would come soon.

Lucia's brows rose in a questioning look. "No offense, but 'dumping' requires actually being a couple."

Holly rolled her eyes at her friend's annoyingly rational logic and ignored the sting her words left behind. How stupid she must look to her friend, pining away over a guy who hadn't been her boyfriend for more than a decade. She took another bite of her croissant. "You know what I mean."

Lucia was watching her as she sipped on her coffee. "Do you want to talk about it?" she asked. Holly smiled at the genuine concern in the other woman's voice. They may not have known each other long but Lucia was rapidly becoming one of her closest friends. Who knew Ivy's scandal would open her world to so many wonderful people?

"You know, I'll probably take you up on that eventually but right now…I'm doing okay."

The truth of those words was surprising. She'd spent the better part of a year planning a life with one man. She'd all but named their imaginary children. But somehow her heart was not broken. She was probably in denial.

Lucia's eyes sparkled with laughter. "I'd say you're better than okay." She sipped her coffee with impossibly wide eyes in feigned innocence. Holly rolled her eyes but she was laughing. Of course her friend wouldn't let this go that easily.

She could hear the shower running and had a searing image of Jack naked in the shower. A thrill ran through her. She knew exactly what he looked like naked.

Now was not the time to be reminiscing about last night's debauchery.

"So what about you," she said in a blatant attempt to turn the conversation away from her and Jack.

"What about me?" Lucia asked, reaching for a croissant.

Holly's eyes narrowed as she studied her friend. Was it her imagination or was Lucia avoiding eye contact. "What brings you to Paris?"

Lucia toyed with the pastry, picking it apart but not eating it. Younger than Holly by several years, Lucia was a fresh-faced beauty with long, wavy dark hair and large, almond-shaped eyes and olive skin. Every time Holly saw her she looked like she'd just stepped off of a runway or out of a shampoo commercial. She was almost always smiling or laughing, a good-natured sweetheart of a girl. Which is why it struck Holly as odd that her friend was avoiding eye contact with a rather grim look on her face.

Holly noticed the circles under the girl's eyes and her unusually pale complexion. "Lucia, is everything all right?"

Lucia looked up at that and gave her a smile that Holly thought was a little forced. "I'll be fine. I just needed to get away for a bit."

Holly was silent, waiting to see if Lucia would continue. After several seconds of silence Lucia sighed. "It's nothing, really. Marco and I just had a fight and my family has been a bit…suffocating, that's all."

Marco was Lucia's fiancé. From what she'd learned from Lucia and Ivy, she knew that the two had been together forever. Their parents were old friends and they had started dating at a young age. Holly had met Marco at the wedding briefly but all she could tell was that he was handsome as sin.

"Do you want to talk about it?" Holly said, unintentionally echoing Lucia's words.

Lucia grinned. "Nope. I'd rather hear more about you and the hottie in the shower," she said, wiggling her eyebrows in a comically suggestive way.

Holly couldn't help it, she burst out laughing. "I'm promise you, there's nothing to tell. It was a one-time thing."

"Mmm-hmm," Lucia said. She raised one brow and was looking at Holly as though she'd just tried to tell her that the Pope was no longer Catholic.

"What, it's true." She and Lucia went back to eating in silence for a moment and when Holly looked up it was to see her friend quietly giggling into her coffee.

"What?" she demanded.

Lucia's amusement seemed to grow. "Nothing, it's just that…it seems you took that saying to heart."

"What saying?" Holly asked.

"The best way to get over a man is to get under another," Lucia said through a fit of laughter.

Holly gasped in mock outrage and threw a small piece of croissant at her friend, who ducked.

* * * *

Jack found the two women in the kitchen a little while later, giggling hysterically and brushing crumbs off of themselves.

"Did I miss a food fight?" he asked.

Holly looked up in surprise. "Something like that," she said before making eye contact with Lucia and laughing all over again.

He watched her for a moment with what he was sure was a goofy grin plastered on his face. He couldn't help it. It was amazing to see Holly laughing. It was a relief to see her happy in general but he was so relieved that she hadn't reverted back to the heartbroken state he'd seen her in last night. Or worse, riddled with guilt or remorse about their night together. But if her easy laughter was anything to go by, Holly was feeling just fine.

A tightness he hadn't realized was gripping his chest since they woke up this morning slowly began to ease. He'd spent the entire shower mentally kicking himself for sleeping with her. Not that he could bring himself to actually regret it. There was no way he would take back last night for anything in the world. It may have been the single most amazing night of his life. But he didn't know what he would have done if she'd regretted it.

But here she was, happy as could be expected, from the looks of it. Maybe their night together had helped. She'd needed a distraction and he was just the sort of no-strings-attached kind of guy to provide it.

She looked up then and caught his eye. He was fairly certain the room was still right-side up but for a moment there he'd lost his balance. *Oh this could not be good.* She was breathtaking. Still wearing his shirt, she'd thrown on a pair of jeans for propriety's sake and was kicking back at the kitchen table like she'd just gotten off the set of a Victoria's Secret photoshoot.

He wasn't sure how long he stood there staring at Holly like an infatuated teen when Lucia spoke, bringing him back to reality. "So how did you find the missing schoolteacher?" she teased, ignoring Holly's eye rolling.

"It wasn't too hard," he said. "I just went around asking if anyone had seen a crazy blonde on a wild goose chase. Word spreads quickly in this city." He looked over at Holly to see how she would take some ribbing about the Benjamin situation and was relieved to find her laughing along with Lucia. Maybe she wasn't as heartbroken as he'd feared.

Or maybe she was a better actress than he realized.

"So what brings you here?" he asked Lucia. "Where's Marco?" Lucia's smile fell a bit and Holly shot him a warning look over Lucia's shoulder. She shook her head a bit and mouthed, "Don't go there."

"I mean, do you have any plans while you're here?" he continued, trying to extract the foot he'd apparently stuck in his mouth.

Lucia's bright smile returned. "Actually, I do. I got tickets to a designer friend's show on Friday night. They are rolling out a new line and it sounds amazing."

Brunelli had mentioned his granddaughter's passion for fashion design many times over the past year they'd been working together and Jack knew it was a point of contention for the old man. He was grooming her to take over the family business and grudgingly accepted that she used all of her spare time pursuing artistic endeavors.

"You guys should come with me," Lucia said, her eyes already lit up with excitement.

"What time is the show?" Holly hedged.

"It starts at seven," she said. "Why do you guys already have big plans?"

Holly looked to him and he scratched at the five o'clock shadow he hadn't gotten around to shaving. "Well, uh, actually," he stalled. He let out a breath. "We're supposed to have dinner with my parents."

Lucia's eyebrows shot up in surprise. "Oh, I hadn't realized you had family here."

"Yeah, well, my brother and his wife live here and my parents are visiting."

Lucia nodded and turned to Holly. "What about you? Do you want to join?"

Holly's nose scrunched up and Jack had to bite back inappropriate laughter as he watched her struggle to find words. "Actually, I have to go to dinner with Jack's family, too. They, uh, they think that we're...."

"A couple," Jack finished for her. Lucia spun in her seat to face Jack and then back to look at Holly.

"You're kidding me," she said.

"But we're definitely *not*," Holly was quick to assure her. A little too quick, Jack thought. She sounded like it was the worst possible idea of all time.

He thought to the conversation they'd had about what they wanted out of life. All right, so it *would* be a bad idea, but she didn't have to sound quite so horrified.

He listened as Holly gave a very brief account of the night before.

"So they think that you guys are a couple even though you're not," Lucia clarified. "But you're going to let them believe that for a little while to spare everyone's feelings and to make Jack look good."

At that last bit she turned to Jack with a look of rueful disdain. "Really, Jack? Again?"

Holly made a snorting noise and he looked over to see her smothering a laugh. "Excuse me, but who got us into this mess in the first place?" he asked her. She immediately threw a hand over her mouth and gave him a wide-eyed look of innocence.

Lucia just shook her head and sighed. "I don't know what it is with you Sinclair women."

Holly's hand dropped and she turned quickly to Lucia. "Don't tell Ivy," she said.

Now it was Jack's turn to laugh at her. "Oh what a tangled web we weave," he teased. She cocked her head to the side and addressed Lucia while she stared at him. "But feel free to tell Danny and your grandfather... and let them know that this was all Jack's idea."

Jack stopped laughing. "Hey, wait a second," he started, but Holly was already out of her chair and heading toward the hallway.

Once she left, he found himself face to face with Lucia who was watching him with crossed arms and narrowed eyes.

He settled into the seat across from her, resigned to hearing a lecture. "Okay, let's hear it. Tell me why this is the worst idea of all time."

Lucia raised an eyebrow. "I think you know the answer to that already."

He did. This wasn't fair to Holly and she would end up—

"You're going to get hurt," Lucia finished.

He stared at her in surprise for a minute. Did she say.... "Wait, you're worried that *I'm* going to get hurt?"

He watched his young friend's forehead wrinkle as she tipped her head, giving him a sympathetic look. That look was answer enough. A panicky feeling took hold of him. For a moment, he felt like Lucia could see something in him that he couldn't. The way she was studying him reminded him of the eerie way his mother would know he was in trouble long before the principal called.

He toyed with the remains of Holly's breakfast. "Holly is the one you should be worried about. She had a rough talk with her—" he struggled to find a word for Benjamin.

"Her infatuation?" Lucia suggested.

"Yeah," he continued. "Did she tell you?" He leaned back and tried not to look too eager but he couldn't deny that there was a part of him that felt like he was in junior high and he wasn't above passing notes in class.

Lucia was watching him closely, her eyes trained on him in a way that was unnerving. He'd never noticed how similar she was to her grandfather until that moment. If he didn't know better, he would think she was scheming.

Chapter 9

Holly watched her friend hold up a dress in front of the mirror. It was the third store they'd been to that afternoon and Lucia was no closer to finding the perfect outfit for the fashion show than when they'd started.

"I like that one," she said, crossing her fingers that this shopping expedition might be coming to an end.

Lucia met her gaze in the mirror and rolled her eyes. "For a summer outing, maybe, but not for a fashion show where I'll be meeting some of the biggest designers in the industry."

Holly plopped down on a settee in the dressing room. "You're not just going as a bystander on Friday, are you?"

Lucia shook her head, her eyes sparkling with mischief. "The designer likes my work. She's promised to introduce me to some key contacts." Lucia picked up another dress from the rack and turned to her with a surprisingly serious expression. "Don't tell my grandpa."

Holly shook her head. "No, of course not. And you…" she started.

Lucia waved away her concerns before she could even start. "Don't worry, I already promised Jack that your secret is safe with me."

"Which one?" she asked. "The fact that we're pretending to be a couple or that we, uh, we…."

Lucia was watching her in the mirror with a grin. "Had a moment?" she offered.

"Yes, exactly, that we had a moment."

Somehow "had a moment" didn't seem to encapsulate the epic passion of the night before but it was the perfect way of putting it because while it may have been mind-blowing, they both knew that it was just a moment. A one-time deal. There was no future for them and they both knew it.

She looked up to see Lucia staring at her in the mirror. "Are you sure you know what you're doing?"

For a second Holly thought Lucia had read her mind. Did she know what she was doing? No. Not a clue. To her friend she said, "Look, we're both adults. We know what we got ourselves into. I needed companionship and Jack….well, Jack…"

What did Jack need? She had been so consumed with her own feelings the night before, so focused on needing something or someone to take her mind off of Benjamin's rejection, it had never occurred to her to question Jack's motivation.

A nagging sense of guilt gnawed at her but she shoved it aside. She'd been battling that vague sensation since she'd left Jack's bed. Part of it had to do with Benjamin. It was hard to go from imagining a life with someone to being intimate with another man without some complicated emotions. But if she was being honest with herself, she didn't so much feel guilt about Benjamin as she felt guilty over how *not* guilty she felt.

She let out a heavy sigh as she watched Lucia head back into a dressing room stall with yet another dress. Feeling guilt over not feeling guilty was ludicrous. She knew that. But now, there was the added layer of unease over the situation with Jack. She wasn't worried that he would get hurt, he was a big boy and he'd made it very clear that he didn't do relationships. Still, she'd never really used a guy before and that was exactly what she'd done the night before. Not that she'd heard him complaining. She caught a glimpse of her reflection in the mirror and caught herself smirking like a prepubescent tween. She shook her head at her reflection. Would she ever grow up? Probably not.

The uneasy pit in her stomach nearly swallowed her alive. There it was. That was the source of the guilt. Who needed a therapist when one could sit idle in a dressing room for hours on end?

Benjamin had been right all along. Things got tough for her and Benjamin and how did she try to fix it? By running off to Paris. And now she'd gone and proven him right again. He didn't think she was capable of settling down so what had she done? Gone and slept with the closest available male.

Way to prove 'em wrong, Holiday. Tears pricked the back of her eyes and she tilted her head back and blinked rapidly, trying to keep them from falling. She would *not* lose it. Not in a dressing room and not when her friend was so excited about this fashion show.

She took a deep, steadying breath but it was too late, her mind had taken a treacherous turn and her thoughts were careening down a one-way street of self-recrimination. Images of the family she had envisioned flashed before her eyes. *Say goodbye to that dream.*

The life she'd planned for herself and Benjamin suddenly seemed completely delusional. Had he known that all along? Of course he had, that's why he'd been so wary. He'd been waiting for her to wake up from her daydream and face reality. She had never been and would never be the kind of woman he settled down with because she was incapable of settling down. Maybe she and Jack were a match made in heaven, after all. They could have one-night stands in passing as they flitted about the globe from one meaningless fling to the next.

She had a flash of Jack leaning over her with that squinty-eyed Tom Cruise grin and let out a soft laugh even as a tear slid down her cheek. It wasn't exactly the worst fate she could imagine.

"What are you laughing about out here?" Lucia asked as she came out wearing another, even more stunning, designer gown.

Holly wiped away the tell-tale tear and smiled at her friend. "That is it, Lucia. You have found the winner."

* * * *

They got back to the apartment a little while later to find Jack absorbed in work. He looked startled when they walked in but his face broke into a grin at the sight of them in the living room doorway.

"Was your mission successful?" he asked.

Holly plopped down on the couch beside him and dropped her head back with a moan, "This woman is a slave driver. Three hours of shopping but it was a success. This little Italian will be the belle of the ball on Friday night."

Lucia laughed as she tossed her packages onto the armchair across from them. "This belle needs to start getting ready. I'm meeting one of my college friends for dinner tonight."

When Lucia left, they were all alone and for a moment the silence was overbearing. Holly couldn't remember the last time she'd felt nervous but sitting there, in the cold light of day, she couldn't deny the butterflies that were swarming in her stomach. She'd all but thrown herself at him last night and now he thought…he must have thought….

"So, about last night," she started.

"I think maybe we should talk," he said at the same time.

Their eyes locked and they both burst out laughing. "Okay, you first," she said.

He turned to her with an unexpectedly serious look. "I just wanted to make sure you felt okay about last night. I hope you know I never intended to take advantage of you or your situation—"

She held up a hand to stop him. "Pretty sure you got it all wrong, mister. You didn't take advantage of me, I took advantage of you."

She saw his lips twitch as his eyes narrowed into a thoughtful stare. "Is that right?" he mused.

She gave a decisive nod. "That's right."

Jack leaned back against the back of the couch. "I don't know how I feel about that."

She cocked a brow. "You seemed to feel just fine about it last night."

His laugh made her stomach do a flip flop. When he reached out a hand to pull her in toward him, she gasped in surprise. She was pressed against his side, their faces inches apart when he asked, "And what about you? Do you feel okay about it?"

Despite his teasing tone, she knew he was serious. His eyes flickered over her face and she saw the hint of anxiety in his eyes. She dropped the joking tone and laid a hand on his chest, feeling the strong, steady beat of his heart. "I feel more than fine," she said. He raised his brows and widened his eyes in a hopeful look and her heart gave a little squeeze. He'd been worried about her, worried that she regretted it.

"Believe me," she said. "My eyes were wide open last night."

He reached out a hand to brush a curl out of her face and she felt a jolt of electricity at the touch. "Do you want to talk about it?"

She knew he was talking about Benjamin and she shook her head quickly. The last thing she wanted to do was talk about him.

She saw the lines around his eyes tighten and his lips pressed together. Uh oh. Jack was having a crisis of conscience. "Look, Holly, I think you should know that I...I don't really do relationships and I don't want—"

Holly couldn't help it. She burst out laughing and Jack's mouth dropped open in surprise. "I'm sorry," she said, still smiling at the shock on his face. "It's just...you don't need to give me the whole 'it's not you, it's me' speech."

"I wasn't going to," he said, sounding offended. "I just wanted to be clear."

"Mmm-hmm." She reached her hands out and placed them on his cheeks, turning his head so he was looking at her. "And I'm just saying, it's not necessary. I know your reputation and I'm totally fine with it."

He looked like he might continue to warn her off so she didn't give him the chance. "I'm a big girl, Jack. I'm not the naïve small-town girl you seem to think I am. And I'm not Ivy—I don't live in a world of black and white."

His eyes darkened and her heart rate quadrupled at the sudden shift in mood. He tugged her again so she was pressed up against him so tightly her breasts rubbed against his chest and his lips were so close she could feel his breath on her lips.

"So what kind of girl are you?" he teased. The flirtatious tone made her feel naughty and alive. A rush of adrenaline pulsed through her, adding to the heat that had her tingling from head to toe. What kind of girl was she?

"The kind who likes adventure," she said.

"Oh yeah?" He leaned in so his lips caressed hers in a feather-light kiss. She nearly moaned aloud at the sweet temptation. Instead she moved into him, capturing his lips with her own and teasing his lips with her tongue.

All restraint gone, his lips moved against hers in an urgency that only heightened the fire between them. Her hand slid down his chest and started to undo his belt. She was wanton with desire, the need to feel him inside of her again and feel his hot skin pressed against her own.

His hand gently stopped hers. He pulled back slightly. "Lucia could walk in," he whispered, his voice cutting into the hazy fog of desire. She muttered a curse and moved back. Pulling away from him was like fighting gravity.

"So now what?" she asked.

He looked at her blankly for a moment and she noticed his eyes were still glazed over with desire. Well, at least she wasn't the only one.

"Maybe I should go get us a hotel room," he said.

She couldn't stop the giggle that escaped her. "I meant us."

"Oh, right." He ran a hand through his hair and visibly tried to pull it together. "What do you want to happen next?"

Holly leaned back a bit and said truthfully, "I want Lucia to head to her dinner so we can finish what we started."

His answering grin was so devilishly sexy it took all of her willpower not to throw herself back into his arms. Only the fact that Lucia could walk in at any moment kept her at a safe distance. "And in the meantime? How does Ms. Adventure want to kill the time? Do you want to go out on the town? See some more of Paris?"

Holly cocked her head to the side and considered her options. "Not to be a total killjoy, but Lucia seriously tired me out this afternoon. I think I just want to stay in tonight."

He settled back in the couch and deftly moved her so she was leaning against him as he flipped on the television and found an old black and white movie that was in English. He moved his head so his mouth was dangerously close to her ear and his breath tickled the side of her neck. "A night in sounds good to me." With one arm tucked around her, his fingers trailed over her arm, sending a shiver down her spine.

His touch was torturously sweet and Holly felt compelled to give as good as she got. Turning so she could whisper in his ear the way he'd done to her, she said, "Don't worry, once Lucia leaves, I'll show you how adventurous I can be."

She felt his body's instant reaction to those words and shot him a victorious grin. He retaliated by moving his wandering hand to her waist where his fingers found the edge of her T-shirt and slid underneath so his fingers were lightly brushing against her bare skin.

By the time Lucia left, Holly thought she might go crazy with desire. Every nerve ending was screaming for more. His soft caresses and whispers were teasing. The moment the front door slammed shut behind Lucia, Holly pounced. Moving so she could straddle Jack, her breath caught at the dark desire in his eyes. He looked dazed—drugged, even— as he ran a hand through her curls and tugged her head toward him in a crushing kiss that left her breathless.

They moved with frantic urgency, tugging at clothes and tearing away every bit of fabric that kept them separate. Holly gasped for air once they were finally bare and his hot skin was pressed against her. He rolled so she was trapped beneath him and she moaned at the sweet torture when he pressed against her, so close but not yet inside her.

He leaned down until his forehead touched hers and she heard him struggling to catch his breath. "I can't wait much longer."

Incapable of forming words, she clutched him to her as she raised her hips, taking him inside of her. His body shuddered as his tight restraint gave way and with a low growl he thrust inside of her over and over again, deeper and harder until she lost herself completely in mindless passion. Shortly after she came apart in his arms, he groaned her name before collapsing on top of her, a warm, cozy blanket of heat as she basked in the afterglow.

* * * *

Jack watched her sleep for a little while—until he realized that if he stared much longer he would be entering into creeper territory. He didn't want to wake her. Not yet. She'd had a rough couple of days and the emotional strain was clearly taking its toll. He gently stroked her hair and she murmured something softly before turning into him and nuzzling against his neck.

He allowed himself a moment to revel in the sweet contentment of having her in his arms but gently pulled away before he started overthinking it. It was post-sex hormones that had him getting all sentimental and attached, he reminded himself. But still, he couldn't remember a time when he'd felt more content. More...complete.

He nearly laughed aloud at the sappy thought. Maybe Lucia had been right, after all. Maybe he was the one he should be worried about. Clearly Holly was well aware there was no hope for a relationship. His lips tugged up in a rueful smile at the memory of her loud laughter when he'd tried to warn her that this couldn't be serious.

What an idiot he'd been. Of course she didn't want a relationship with him. She'd made it abundantly clear that she didn't want him. Well, not like that, at least. All Holly needed from him was fun and distraction— two things he happened to excel at.

Gently prying himself from her loose embrace, Jack threw on his clothes and tip-toed from the room.

By the time Holly woke a half hour later, Jack had already returned from the corner store and was lighting candles on the table he'd set up on the balcony. He looked up at the sound of Holly's voice in the doorway.

"What are you doing out here?"

She looked so unbelievably adorable, standing there all tousled and sleepy, for a moment Jack thought his heart had stopped beating. Then it kicked into overdrive as if he'd just run a marathon.

"Hey sleepyhead," he said. "I thought you might be hungry for dinner."

He pulled out a chair and she gave him a little smile that seemed almost...shy. She slid into the seat without a word as she stared at the spread he'd set out, taking in the candles and champagne and the array of bread, cheese, and meats. She blinked a couple of times but remained speechless. This was a side of Holly he'd never seen before.

For a minute he thought maybe she was upset. Or maybe he'd crossed some boundary. They had agreed to keep this casual, after all, maybe a romantic dinner on the balcony made her uncomfortable. When she finally spoke, her voice was quiet but her smile was brilliant. "Thank you, Jack. This is....this is perfect."

And it was perfect. They spent the next few hours talking and laughing about everything and nothing. As if they'd made some sort of unspoken agreement, neither of them brought up Benjamin or anything that might mar the festive atmosphere. Instead they shared stories from their pasts, which soon turned into a competition over who had been more wild as a child or, even more entertaining, as a teen.

They were laughing so hard by the time Lucia came home, they didn't hear her enter until she was standing in the doorway. Taking one look at the empty champagne glasses and the remains of dinner, Lucia lifted a brow. "Am I interrupting?"

She looked to Jack and he knew without a doubt that she was reading more into this than she should. "Not at all, come join us."

The three of them talked until they were yawning too much to continue. Saying their goodnights, Jack watch Holly head to her room before going to his…alone.

* * * *

Holly knew she should stay in her own room. She and Jack may be sleeping together but they were not *sleeping* together. They hadn't actually written down the rules but everyone knew that casual flings did not spend the night. Well, unless one was too tired out from sex to make it to his or her own bed. But this was different. Holly tossed and turned. Her mind, which she'd pleasantly distracted all day long, had switched into overdrive the moment she tried to close her eyes and go to sleep.

For someone who had always lived life on a whim—for whom the term "life plan" had always been a laughable phrase—she had gotten terribly attached to hers. Suddenly a future that she'd seen before her, clear as a picture, was replaced by a dark, hazy void. What would she do now that Benjamin rejected her?

There was no reason to stay in Oakdale. But then again, if she was going to settle down, her hometown was as good a choice as any. At least she'd be close to family. And Benjamin. She heaved a sigh at the thought of running into Benjamin on a regular basis—a constant reminder of the dream life she'd never have. Maybe she wouldn't stay in Oakdale after all. All she knew was, she didn't want to keep living the nomadic life she'd been leading. Not that she wanted to give up the travel altogether but she wanted some sort of stability. An anchor, to keep her rooted in place. She would never give up the dream for a family—the miscarriage and now the aching jealousy she felt whenever she spoke to her sister had made it all too clear what was missing in her life.

Try as she might, she couldn't shake the dream she'd been clinging to this past year, nor could she picture a new reality for herself. Benjamin was her family—her future—he was her anchor. Without him keeping her grounded, she could never have the life she'd planned. She'd never have that stability. That thought brought a fresh wave of sadness.

Exhausted and desperately in need of sleep to turn off her brain, Holly finally gave into temptation. Tiptoeing out of her bedroom and down the hall, she paused outside of Jack's closed door. She was dangerously close to crossing a line here. But the thought or returning to her cold, lonely bed was depressing and he was right there, so close. Besides, they'd already agreed that this wasn't going anywhere. He wouldn't read into it any more than she would.

With that thought in mind, she opened the door and headed toward the bed. He looked so adorable lying fast asleep. He woke when she sat on the side of the bed. "Holly?" he murmured. "Are you okay?"

Holly nodded. She didn't want to talk. "I'm fine. But can I…um, can I sleep in here tonight?"

Jack's eyes were half open and for a moment he stared at her as though confused. But then a slow, sleepy grin spread across his face and he tugged her hand so she was lying beside him. Then, in one quick move, he'd tucked her into him and curled around her so she was buried in a warm, safe cocoon that smelled amazingly good.

He nuzzled her neck through her hair until his lips reached her skin. Giving her a little kiss, he asked, "Better?"

Holly could only manage a quiet moan of contentment. She was already slipping into a deep, dreamless sleep.

The next morning, she woke feeling well rested and mildly confused as to where she was. Then she spotted Jack, typing away on his laptop at the desk in the corner. "Morning," he said once he noticed that she was awake.

"Morning." She pushed her curls out of her face and clutched the cover to her body, which was overkill since she was fully clothed as it was. She was slightly mortified. More uncomfortable than she'd felt when she'd woken in his bed naked the day before. Waking up in a man's bed after a night of lovemaking was one thing. But she had crawled into his bed for cuddles. *Cuddles*, for the love of God. What had she been thinking? He was already worried that she wanted more from him and now he must be convinced that she was some kind of needy chick who wanted him to be her boyfriend.

Still typing at the computer, he said, "Lucia went out, she said something about helping one of her designer friends before the fashion show tomorrow. She wanted you to join her but we both figured you'd rather get some sleep."

She blinked at his back in confusion. "What time is it?"

"Almost noon."

Holly sat up straight. "What? Why did you let me sleep that long?" *And in your room? Ugh.* She whipped off the covers and starting to get out of bed.

Jack looked over in surprise before joining her on the bed, effectively pinning her back down to the mattress. "Hey, what's your hurry? You clearly needed sleep and it's not like you had any obligations today. You're on vacation, remember?"

He was smiling down at her and the tension that had filled Holly's chest started to ease. He didn't seem put out in the slightest that they'd cuddled the night away. In fact, he seemed pretty damn pleased with himself.

Eyes sparkling with excitement, he rolled over in the bed so he could grab a box from the nightstand. "I got you something."

Holly sat upright. "You got me something?" she repeated. "When did you do that?"

"This morning," he said. "While you were sleeping."

"Oh." It was oddly strange to think of him coming in and out of the bedroom, going about his life, all while she slept in a coma, apparently, in his bed. It was even stranger to think that he'd gone out to buy her a present.

"Jack, you shouldn't have," she started. When she took the box from him, she looked up at him in surprise. "A phone?"

She didn't know what she'd been expecting, but a phone was definitely not it.

"It's a prepaid with international service," he explained. He was looking so proud of himself, Holly couldn't help but smile back at him.

"Thank you, but you really didn't have to do that. You don't have to get me presents."

Jack sat beside her, leaning against the wall. "I know, but it's not so much a present for you as it is for Ivy."

Holly's head snapped up at that. "For Ivy?"

Jack nodded. "I know that she hates when she can't get a hold of you so I thought—"

Holly's sigh cut him off. "I know, she worries about me." It was the story of her life. Her parents and Ivy and their older brothers were forever worrying about her.

Jack's brows were furrowed in confusion for a second before understanding dawned. "Oh no, that's not what I meant. Ivy needs you, now more than ever. And she's going to need you even more once the baby arrives. I just wanted her to have a way of getting a hold of you."

Holly stared at him for so long, he started to shift in the bed, clearly uncomfortable. But Holly didn't know what to say. His words had struck something in her. *She needs you.* She'd never thought of it like that. She wasn't sure anyone else saw their relationship that way but the fact that Jack did made her choked up and giddy with joy all at the same time.

How had she never seen that before? She and her sister had always been close but it always seemed like their relationship revolved around Ivy helping Holly. That was just the way it was. But now….

Her brain went from one scenario to another when Ivy had called her for advice or just to vent over the past couple of years. *She needed her.*

Jack was still watching her warily and she hoped none of the silly sentimentality was visible in her smile. "Thanks, Jack. Really. That means a lot."

He gave her the squinty grin before tackling her back to the mattress, which left her breathless with laughter. "That's what friends are for, right?" he teased.

Holly giggled. "Mmm-hmm." She slipped a hand down toward the erection that was pressing against her thigh through his jeans. "And this is what friends with benefits are for," she said as she stroked the length of him.

His groan sent shivers down her spine. "My God, Holly," he whispered. "You are such a good friend."

Chapter 10

Jack couldn't remember when he'd had more fun. In fact, he didn't think he'd ever had so much fun in his entire life. When they finally left the bed, Holly led him on a whirlwind tour of the city. They visited her favorite neighborhoods and traipsed through narrow cobblestone streets, occasionally dropping into stores and frequently stopping at patisseries "for energy" as Holly put it.

By the end of the day, Jack had learned two things—Holly made everything fun. Everything. Even shoe shopping. And she ran solely on sugar and caffeine.

By the time Lucia met up with them for a late dinner, Jack was exhausted and his face hurt from smiling. Which was why, when Holly casually mentioned that she would be heading to Italy soon over dinner, Jack froze with his fork halfway to his mouth.

"What? Why?" His voice may have been a tad to plaintive because Holly and Lucia both gave him a funny look. Holly seemed confused but Lucia seemed almost…pitying. Oh crap. That's not what he meant.

"I mean, I know you have to be there for Ivy," he continued. "But there's no rush, is there?"

Holly's nose scrunched up as she considered him. "You mean other than the baby who may make an appearance any day now?"

Jack cleared his throat. Right. That. "I just meant, Ivy or Daniel will call when it's time and…"

Holly gave him a knowing grin. "This is about your parents, isn't it?"

Jack drew a blank. What was she talking about? Before he could respond, she continued. "Don't worry, Jack. I'll stick around until after we have dinner with your parents." She gave him a light, friendly punch in the arm. A punch in the arm? Seriously? They had slept together multiple times—multiple, *amazing* times, in fact.

Some of the joy he'd been reveling in began to fade as he realized she was serious about leaving in two days. He'd known this wasn't going to last forever—that was the point of a casual fling—but still, he'd thought he had more than a day and a half.

He barely paid attention to the conversation after that. And since the conversation was about the designers Lucia was working with and the fashion show the following night, neither woman seemed to expect him to contribute much anyway.

It wasn't until they were back at the apartment and Lucia went to bed that Jack brought it up again. They were alone on the balcony, enjoying the cool breeze and twinkling lights. "Are you really in such a hurry to leave this?" he asked, gesturing to the view.

Holly smiled over at him. "I hate to leave, but it's time I get back to reality." She let out a little sigh, "Don't get me wrong, Jack. This has been..." her voice trailed off and he found himself waiting eagerly for her to finish. What? It had been fun? Amazing? Breathtaking? She never finished. Instead she just smiled again, though her eyes held sadness. "But this isn't reality. I can't keep hiding from my life."

Jack took a deep breath and nodded slowly. He could understand that. By staying here she was putting off talking to her sister and the rest of her family.

"I need to figure out where I'm going next or if I want to stay in Oakdale," she continued. "And I need to talk to Benjamin."

Jack's head snapped up at the mention of the other man's name. They had both studiously avoided talking about him ever since the first time they slept together. He still hated the name. More than ever, in fact.

"I thought you said it was over," he said.

She shrugged. She was staring off into the distance and he wished she would look his way. He wanted to see what emotions were playing out in her eyes. "That's what he said," she answered. "But it doesn't feel resolved, you know? There's still so much to be said."

Like what? He wanted to ask. But a part of him realized he didn't want to hear the answer. If she was planning on begging him to come back, he didn't want to know.

Instead he found himself saying, "Do you think he'll change his mind?" When she didn't immediately answer, he added, "Do you want him to?"

That got her attention. She turned to him then with a bittersweet smile. She ignored the last question but answered the first. "I think it's possible that he'll change his mind. People do it all the time." He saw her inhale deeply and knew she was hurting despite the smile. "I did. I mean, I used to think I would never settle down. I thought I would always want to be carefree, no responsibilities, no commitments. But then I...I changed my mind."

There was a deeper sadness in her eyes that he would give anything to erase. He hadn't missed the hitch in her voice when she was talking. Something or someone had made her change her mind. Whatever it was, she clearly didn't want to talk about it. He reached out a hand and placed it on her arm and she squeezed it.

Shaking her head as though shaking off the memories, she asked lightly, "So what about you? Do you think you'll ever change your mind?"

"About?" he asked, though he knew exactly what she was referring to.

Her eyes narrowed as she studied him. She knew he was being intentionally obtuse. "Do you think you'll ever change your mind about commitment, relationships, family..." She made a vague gesture as her voice trailed off.

His chest tightened at the question. He didn't want to answer. He had a cache of witty comebacks that he used whenever anyone asked him if he would ever settle down but right now they all seemed insincere and shallow—completely inappropriate in the wake of her honest emotions.

So he said the truth. "It wouldn't be a good idea."

She blinked at him in surprise. "What do you mean?"

He lifted a shoulder in a halfhearted shrug. "Ask my family what they think about me procreating," he said with a laugh. "You'll get an earful of reasons why it wouldn't work. Hell, ask Danny or Brunelli, they'll tell you why it's a terrible idea."

Holly tilted her head as she studied him. Setting her chin in a stubborn expression he was coming to know well she leaned back in her chair with her arms crossed. "I'm not asking them, I'm asking you."

He tried to think of a good response but his mind was annoyingly blank.

She leaned forward and stared at him with an intensity that was unnerving. "You know what I think, Jack? I think you and I have pigeonholed ourselves. We created these identities when we were younger and now that's how everyone sees us."

He noticed the unusually serious look in her eyes and the way her lips were tight with emotion. She was passionate about this and it seemed crucial to her that he understand. He thought about what she'd said and realized the truth in it. He had spent the better part of his life playing the role of the carefree playboy—the cocky, unpredictable, unreliable rogue. It had gotten to the point where he didn't know where the role ended and he began.

"Maybe you're right," he said. He forced a smile despite the tightness in his chest. "But maybe I like who I am. Maybe I don't want to change."

She didn't return his smile. Not right away at least. He could feel a tension build between them that he hated. But it was also a relief. A panicky feeling of expectation had begun to form and he couldn't face it. Not yet.

Finally she returned his smile and her laugh was self-deprecating. "You're right," she said. "I guess sometimes reputations come about for a reason. Of course you don't want to change that and why should you? You've got the world eating out of the palm of your hand. Any guy would trade places with you."

Jack returned her smile but the warm contentment he'd experienced for the past two days was rapidly cooling and there was an empty pit in his gut when he considered her words. Any guy would trade places with him, she'd said. Something told him there was one man who wouldn't—Benjamin.

When it was time to head to bed, he tugged her hand, pulling her into his room. She didn't argue and when the door closed and he pulled her into his arms, she went willingly. Eagerly. When they made love there was an urgency between them, an emotional connection that had never been there before.

* * * *

Lucia was like a dog with a bone. The two women had gone out to get some groceries for lunch and Lucia had spent the entire outing grilling Holly on the Jack situation. That's what Lucia was now calling it. "The Jack Situation." "It's not a 'situation'," Holly explained. "It's just..." What was it, exactly? Because she had no idea. "Fling" didn't seem right, not with the amount of talking and laughing and...connecting... that had gone on between them over the past few days. But, at the same time, it wasn't like they were dating. He had made that abundantly clear many times over.

Her mind drifted back to her big mouth the night before when she'd called him out on his reputation. What had she been thinking? She'd been kicking herself all day for being *that girl*.

He'd been nothing but honest with her from the very beginning. He wasn't looking for a relationship. She was fine with that. But for a brief moment there when she'd been talking about changing one's mind, she'd realized that she was talking about Jack and not Benjamin. She was wondering if he would ever change his mind about wanting a family.

She forced a deep breath as she pushed that memory away. It had been a momentary weakness. Still, that little slip up—that emotional snafu—was a great reminder that it was time for her to move on. With or without Benjamin.

With that in mind, she turned to face Lucia as they got on the elevator to the penthouse. "It doesn't matter, anyway. The 'situation' will be over soon. I'm heading back to Italy, remember?"

"I remember," her friend grumbled. "You're running away."

Holly's jaw dropped as she saw her friend's wicked grin. "Am not!"

Lucia rolled her eyes. "Whatever you say, scaredy-cat."

Holly pulled a baguette from the bag she was holding and swatted her friend with it.

The conversation came to a screeching halt once the doors to the suite opened and Jack come toward them to help relieve them of the groceries.

"To be continued," Lucia said under breath before disappearing into the kitchen.

"What was that about?" Jack asked.

Holly widened her eyes to give him an innocent look. "Um, nothing?"

He gave a snort of disbelief but he let it go.

After lunch, they took a walk along the Seine and Holly tried not to get too despondent at the thought of leaving the city. She would be back. Maybe not with Jack and most likely never in such luxury, but she would definitely be back.

They came back to the apartment just as Lucia started getting ready for the fashion show. Jack and Holly still had a little time before dinner with his parents. Her final performance as Jack's girlfriend. After that they planned on meeting up with Lucia at the fashion show after party.

"Penny for your thoughts," Jack said as he flopped down beside her on the couch. "You've been unusually quiet all day."

She gave him the sunniest smile she could muster given the heavy ache that had settled in her chest all day. She drew in a deep breath. "I guess I just haven't had my quota of sugar for the day. That will have to be remedied."

Jack reached a hand out and tugged her against him. "I've got your sugar right here, baby," he said in a comically low voice.

Holly laughed and swatted his hand. "Lucia is in the other room and I have to get ready for dinner." Her grin grew wicked. "I guess dessert will have to wait."

He groaned as she stood up and headed toward the door. "You don't have to run off right away."

When she reached the doorway she turned around to face him, "I have to get ready. I've got to make a good impression on my boyfriend's parents," she said in a sing-song voice.

He grinned at her. "Very funny."

She turned to leave but then poked her head back into the living room as a thought occurred to her. "Mind if I borrow your laptop for a bit? I want to make sure I haven't missed any big news from home."

"It's all yours," he said with a wide wave of his hand.

* * * *

Holly skimmed through her mom's melodramatic emails. As expected, the fact that she'd taken off to France did not go over well at home. Thank God it was Ivy who'd had to listen to the lectures and not her.

Glancing over the slew of junk mail, one name popped out at her. *Benjamin.* Holly's breath caught as her finger hovered over his name debating if she wanted to read it. She'd finally stopped crying and was doing a great job of distracting herself, thanks in no small part to the hottie in the living room. But curiosity won out and she opened the email.

Her mouth went dry and she swallowed compulsively as she read,

Holiday,

I'm so sorry for the way we left things on the phone. You know I've always loved you. You've always been the girl of my dreams and I'd be lying if I said I haven't thought about what it could be like if we gave it another shot. I'm just not sure we should be jumping into something right now. I'd like to take it slow and see what happens. I understand if you don't want to wait. We'll talk more when you get home.

Take care of yourself,

Benjamin

Holly read the note three times in a row before sitting back, one hand clapped over her mouth as she wobbled between excitement and frustration. He wasn't saying no! But he wasn't saying yes, either. So where did that leave them? With hope, she finally decided. At the very least, she had hope that her dreams for the future would come true. And just like that, the daydream that had seemed so preposterous the day before was back in place.

She could do this. Jumping off the bed, she started pacing back and forth in the room. She just had to convince him to give her a chance. They'd talk once she returned, he'd said. Not good enough. Maybe she could buy him a ticket to Italy so he could meet her there. What would be more romantic than a road trip along the Amalfi Coast? And then he'd see her holding Ivy's baby and it would be game over.

She felt a now-familiar twinge at the thought of holding a baby. It had been a year since the miscarriage but it still hurt. She wanted to experience that miracle again…and soon. And with the right man.

There was a quiet knock on her bedroom door before Jack poked his head in. "Hey, you almost ready? We should probably head out soon."

Holly stopped mid-pace. Their dinner plans had totally slipped her mind. "Sorry," she said with an apologetic wince. "I got distracted."

His eyes narrowed a bit and he pursed his lips. "You look…different."

She placed her hands on her hips and cocked her head to the side. She pretended to think about it. "Different, huh? Maybe…happy?"

He walked in slowly. "Yeah, that's it. What's going on?"

She hesitated for a brief moment. Would it be weird to talk about Benjamin with Jack after the past few days? No, of course not, Jack had made it very clear this was not about feelings.

The words came out on a rush of air. "Benjamin emailed last night to apologize. We're getting back together!"

Jack stared at her in surprise. His expression was unreadable. "Back together?"

She rolled her eyes. "Oh all right, maybe that's a stretch. But he wants to talk. He's not ruling us out."

She watched Jack shove his hands in his pockets.

"How romantic." His tone was uncharacteristically caustic.

Holly's spine stiffened. "Why are you being like that?"

"Like what?" he asked, his tone sharp and the charming grin nowhere to be found.

"Like that." She turned her back on him so she could close up his laptop and hand it over. When she went to hand it to him, he didn't immediately take it.

"I think you deserve better," he said. The words came out so quickly, she thought she'd misheard him. When they sank in her throat closed up and she didn't know if she was going to cry or scream.

"What do you know about what I deserve?" She hated how hoarse her voice sounded but she continued on, "You don't know anything about Benjamin. Or me. And you certainly don't know anything about us as a couple."

"How could I, when you're not a couple?" he bit back. "You haven't been for more than a decade, from what I hear."

The words stung but it was the fact that they were coming from Jack that was really painful. She'd thought he'd understood. For some reason she'd come to believe that he understood her in a way that no one else could. They were two peas in a pod. He *got* her. Or at least he was supposed to.

But no, he only got the side of her that she was ready to leave behind. "I wouldn't expect you to understand," she said, the words coming out between stiff lips.

"What's that supposed to mean?"

"It means you've made it very clear how you feel about commitment and grown-up relationships." She moved to the dresser and started to fiddle with her makeup. She picked up her powder before setting it back down. She couldn't concentrate on what she was doing, she was too addled by the fact that they were fighting. *Fighting.* And with Jack, the most laid-back man she'd ever met.

"Is that what you call whatever this is you two are doing? A grown-up relationship?" He moved so he was in her line of sight and she turned to face him head on. His words were getting to her and that only made her more defensive. He had no idea what he was talking about, why was she even listening to him?

"It's more grown up than...." She gestured between the two of them. "This."

He threw his hands up in the air and looked at her like she had lost her mind. "That's because we agreed, this is not a relationship."

"Exactly," she said..

"All right then," he said, his voice still gruff but his volume going back to normal as they moved toward one another.

Her breath was coming hot and heavy as anger and frustration battled with something else. Desire. Goddammit, he was sexy when he was pissed. His brain seemed to be going in the same direction because he took a step closer and his gaze was locked on her lips. She slipped her tongue out to wet her lips and watched as his eyes turned dark with lust.

"What are we fighting about?" he asked.

"I have no idea," she whispered. Her mind was a blank. All she could think of was closing the distance between them and feeling his lips on hers. All it would take was one tiny step forward. She leaned forward and he met her halfway there, his arms pulled her tight against him as their lips met in an urgent, breathless kiss.

A soft knock of the door made her jump back. She stared at him with wide eyed horror as Lucia called through the door. "Everything okay in there? I heard yelling."

Jack wiped a hand over his face and drew in a deep breath. He looked just as rattled as she felt.

"We're fine," Holly called out as she headed toward the door. She opened it to find Lucia looking absolutely stunning in full hair and makeup and a dress that looked like it was made for her hourglass figure. Jack let out a whistle behind her.

"You look amazing, Lucia," he said. She could feel him standing behind her and wished she wasn't so aware of his body in relation to hers.

Lucia was grinning, her eyes twinkling with excitement as she twirled. "Thank you. Now tell me, what's going on?"

Holly glanced back to Jack who said, "Nothing to worry about. Holly and I are just having a difference of opinion."

Lucia looked from Jack to Holly and back again with eyes narrowed in suspicion. Holly had a feeling Lucia wanted to meddle but she kept her mouth shut only making a little "hmmm" noise of disbelief. "Well I'd better go meet up with my friends." She pointed a finger at them. "You two have fun tonight…and try not to kill each other."

Holly held up her pinky. "Pinky swear. I will not kill Jack tonight."

She glanced back at Jack who made of show of rolling his eyes in grudging agreement. "Yeah, yeah. We'll play nice."

Lucia laughed and gave them each a peck on the cheek before heading out.

Left alone once again, Holly thought the silence might drown them. What was going on here? They hadn't known each other long but long enough to know that they did not do awkward silences. Heck, it was amazing they could be in the same room with one another without running out of air. They were both talkers but right now Holly had no idea what to say. Her mind was a blank. Something had changed between them and she had no clue how to make it right.

"Maybe we should talk about what's been going on with us," she said. Even she could hear the distaste in her voice. She didn't want to have to talk about it. That defeated the purpose of a fun fling. But it seemed obvious that they needed to clear the air.

Jack ran a hand through his hair, pushing his hair out of his face. "There's nothing to talk about," he said "We both knew it was a casual thing."

Holly nodded. Good. That was what she was hoping he'd say. She ignored the aching sensation in her chest. Her emotions were all over the place these days, she couldn't be sidetracked by a silly crush.

There it was. She couldn't deny it to herself any longer. She was smitten. But then, in her defense, this was the man she'd had a crush on from afar for the past few years, ever since he'd become a tabloid staple.

He'd been her fantasy man, just like he had been for every other hot-blooded American woman with a penchant for gossip magazines. There was nothing wrong with that and it didn't mean anything.

With that thought in mind, she forced herself to nod. "Right, glad we're on the same page."

He was watching her with a wry smile.

"We just—it can't—" she started. She cleared her throat, which had suddenly gone dry. "It can't happen again."

His grin dropped and he stared at her with an unreadable expression for a moment before saying, "Yeah, sure. That makes sense."

"Not that the last few days weren't great," she rushed to say. "Because they were."

"Obviously," he said, with an over the top smirk that made her laugh despite herself.

"Obviously," she agreed. "But it's just that…" Her eyes drifted to the laptop that Jack had set down on the dresser.

She looked back to see Jack studying her. His eyes were merciless as he read her face and her eyes the same way she'd watched him study the screen of his laptop when he was working. Being the object of that intense scrutiny made her shift from foot to foot.

"I get it," he said at last. "You don't want to feel like you're cheating on Benjamin." She couldn't help but notice the way Benjamin's name sounded like a curse word coming out of Jack's mouth. Was it wrong that there was a little part of her that hoped he was jealous? Probably.

"Thanks for understanding, it's just—"

"I don't understand," he cut in.

"But you just said—"

"I get what you want from me and I'll respect it. But I don't understand why." He was more serious than she'd ever seen him. His brow was furrowed as he continued to study her with a thoughtfulness she suspected few ever witnessed firsthand. She remembered her sister Ivy saying once that there was a serious streak to Jack that most people didn't see. Well now she was one of the few.

She shifted back toward the dresser so she didn't have to face him and toyed with the makeup on the counter again, moving items around for no particular reason. He was waiting for her to speak, to explain.

"I've known Benjamin forever," she started. Then she stopped. And what? That meant they had to be together forever? Even she could see how ludicrous that sounded. She took a deep breath and turned to face him, conscious of the fact that she was explaining her decisions for her own sake as much as his.

"He knows me," she continued. "He knows me inside and out, and he loves me."

Jack's eyebrows rose a bit and she knew what he was thinking. "I mean love in the big sense. Like we're family. He's already my family. So it makes sense that he should be the man who I have a family with."

Jack nodded slowly. "I think that's the problem."

Her hands stilled as her brain instantly came up with defensive arguments against whatever he was about to say. "What's my problem?"

He sighed a bit. "You just said 'it makes sense' when talking about love. In my experience, the two words aren't in the same universe. If it makes sense, it's not love."

Holly's breath caught in her throat. She'd never heard him sound so sincere, so genuine. The honesty in his voice took away any sting his words might have caused and instead she found herself fighting against tears that threatened to choke her. His words struck a chord in her that she couldn't deny.

"I don't expect you to understand," she said. When she turned around she saw that he was looking toward the door, seemingly lost in thought.

"And why's that?" he asked. He didn't sound angry, just…curious. But he wouldn't meet her eyes and she found herself struggling to find words that wouldn't be offensive.

"Because you're not interested in that kind of thing—family and marriage and all that."

He was silent but he turned to look at her then. For some reason she felt like she'd hurt his feelings. "You told me that yourself," she said, as though he'd accused her of lying.

Jack nodded slowly. "Yeah, I guess I did."

She opened her mouth, about to ask him if he'd had a change of heart. Or if that whole playboy side of him was all part of the persona he put on for the press. But before she had a chance, he changed the topic back to her.

"Why is it so important to you? I mean, from what I know of you, you don't exactly strike me as the settle down type either."

Her head snapped back. Did he have any idea how much that hurt? "That's exactly why I'm trying to change."

"Because you want to *settle down*?" His lip curled back in a sneer at the word.

"Why do you say it like that?"

"Like what?"

"Like settling down is a joke."

His eyes widened in shock. "It's right there in the words. You want to settle."

"That's not what I mean and you know it," she said.

He paced before her, shaking his head. "I just don't get it."

The words were out of her mouth before she could stop them. "I had a miscarriage."

The silence was deafening. He stopped pacing to turn and look at her, his forehead creased in concern. "What? When?"

Holly sighed. She hadn't told anyone about the miscarriage, not even Benjamin, and now that the words were out, it was strangely cathartic, like a weight had been lifted from her chest. The pain was still there but it no longer felt so constricting.

"Almost a year ago," she said. "I was in Croatia and sort of dating some guy. Some loser who meant nothing to me and I clearly meant nothing to him." She could hear the bitterness in her voice but couldn't do anything to stop it.

When Jack came toward her, she told herself to push him away—she was trying to keep her distance, that was the whole point of this conversation—but the concern in his eyes was so welcome, she couldn't bring herself to turn away. He reached his arms out and she stepped into them, letting out a sigh of relief at the warmth and comfort she found there.

"I'm sorry," he said, speaking to the top of her head.

She nodded, her head against his chest. "Me too."

Chapter 11

Jack struggled to find words to make her feel better. He'd never known the kind of pain she'd gone through but he'd seen it written all over her face and it had broken his heart. He would do absolutely anything to make her feel better, to make her smile. Even if that meant supporting her stupid plan to win back her old flame. *Benjamin.*

"Does he know?" Jack asked.

"Benjamin?" she asked. Her voice was muffled against his shirt.

Jack was glad she couldn't see him flinch. He hated that guy's name even more coming out of her mouth. "Yeah." He felt her head shake against his chest.

"No."

He wanted to ask "why" but contented himself with stroking her back and listening to the sound of her breathing. He would have been content to stay there all day, he realized with a start. That was odd. And unsettling. But there it was. This woman was getting under his skin.

"So," he continued. "You've decided that Benjamin needs to be the father."

There was a slight pause before he felt her nod. She pushed herself away from him and looked directly into his eyes as she explained. "He's stable and committed and reliable, he's…" her voice trailed off but Jack knew how it would finish. *Everything I'm not.*

Jack nodded, trying to swallow back the frustration he felt over her logic. "So you've decided he's the guy you want to marry even though you don't love him? Don't these hypothetical kids of yours deserve to have two parents who love each other?"

Holly's mouth dropped open and he watched her cheeks turn a pretty shade of pink. At first he thought he'd just surprised her but once she found her voice, it was anger he heard. "I *do* love him, how many times do I have to tell people that?"

"As many times as it takes until you believe it, I suppose." The words came out of Jack's mouth before he could stop them. He clamped his mouth shut at her wide-eyed look of shock. Dammit, he hadn't intended to hurt her. It wasn't his place to tell her who to love and what to do with her life. He shouldn't be involved. This was exactly why he *didn't* get involved.

"Is this because of…us?" she asked. Her eyes had narrowed and she pushed back a little further, so he was at arm's length.

"What?" he snapped. "No, of course not." Her brows pulled together in…oh no, was that concern? Or worse, pity? Oh this was definitely not acceptable. "Look, I'm a big boy, I know these last few days didn't mean anything. That's not what this is about."

Holly crossed her arms in front of her chest and tilted her chin up. "Okay, so what is it about then?"

Jack struggled to find the words. He didn't know why it meant so much to him that she wake up to the truth—preferably before making a monumental mistake—all he knew was, it was imperative that he get through to her.

Before he could come up with any words to explain, she let out a weary sigh and her shoulders slumped. "You know what? I don't want to hear it. People have been telling me reasons why I shouldn't get back together with Benjamin for the past six months, there's nothing you can say that I haven't heard."

Her eyes looked so sad, she looked so…defeated…not at all like the Holly he'd come to know. He couldn't bring himself to argue with her any more. Instead he asked, "And you're sure it has to be him?"

Her eyes met his then and his chest tightened so painfully, for a moment he couldn't breathe. "It's always been him."

The words were a sledgehammer against his chest but he did his best to hide the way they hurt. He had gone into this with eyes wide open and so had she. They were never supposed to be more than a fling. That was what he'd wanted…that's what he always wanted. No strings attached. So when had he gone and fallen for this golden-haired beauty?

* * * *

Dinner was a disaster. No, *he* was a disaster. Holly was perfect in every way. She charmed the socks off of his parents with her glittery smile and her outgoing, upbeat ways. Jack watched in awe as she laughed and asked questions and effortlessly wrapped his parents around her little finger. She was amazing.

It was Jack who was a dud. He caught his mom throwing him curious looks and he couldn't blame her. He wasn't sure he'd ever been so quiet in his entire life. If things were normal, he would be cracking jokes along with Holly, or at the very least, participate in the conversation.

But nothing was normal. Jack's life had been tipped upside down and it was all the fault of his lovely pretend girlfriend who sat by his side—so incredibly close but so very unavailable. What the hell had happened here? At what point had he gone and fallen for his best friend's sister?

His mind flashed on the night of Ivy's wedding. The way he'd held Holly in his arms and it had felt so right. So perfect. Maybe he'd been a goner from the start. Now the question way, what was he going to do about it?

Nothing. The answer was a leaden weight in his gut. He wouldn't do anything about it because he wasn't the man she wanted. More than that, he wasn't even in the right category. She had made it very clear from the beginning what type of guy she was looking for—and it was definitely not him. No one in their right mind would call him stable. Or reliable. Or committed...to anything other than work, at least.

Still. He found it hard to believe that Benjamin was the right man for her. Anyone stupid enough to turn her down or make her doubt that she was anything less than perfect was not right for Holly. So how could he make her see that? How could he get her to move on and find someone more deserving? There had to be a better alternative out there—someone who would appreciate her zest for life and her humor and her passion. Someone who could give her the future she wanted.

He was stewing over how he could make her realize that Benjamin wasn't her only option when his father interrupted his train of thought with a question about his work. He didn't catch the entire question, he'd been so lost in thought.

All eyes were on him and Jack cleared his throat. "Sorry, what?"

His father repeated the question but Jack didn't miss the exchanged looks at the table. "Is everything all right?" his mother asked.

He glanced over to see Holly watching him in concern as well. She raised her eyebrows a bit in question when he looked her way but he shook his head. "Yeah, everything is fine. Sorry, just a bit distracted tonight. I have a major deadline due next week and I guess I'm a little preoccupied."

That seemed to be enough to keep his parents from prying any further but he was well aware of Holly's eyes on him for the rest of the meal.

* * * *

Jack was acting weird. Like *weird*-weird. Ever since their little showdown in her bedroom that afternoon, he had been acting strange. If she didn't know any better, she would think he was nervous.

But she did know better, Jack was not someone who got nervous or flustered or even tongue-tied. There had to be something big going on if he was acting like this around his parents.

By the time they'd said goodbye to his parents Holly was ready to pounce. "What's going on with you?" she asked the moment his parents walked out of view.

Jack shrugged but he wouldn't look in her direction as they headed toward the curb to hail a taxi. "I don't know what you're talking about."

Holly stopped in the middle of the sidewalk, forcing pedestrians to veer around her and Jack to stop and look back. She planted her hands on her hips. "You don't know what I'm talking about?" she echoed.

He was facing her but Holly noticed with alarm that he still wasn't making eye contact. Oh this couldn't be good. She walked up to him, stopping only when they were practically touching. She reached up and held his face between her hands, forcing him to look at her. "You were acting weird at dinner," she said. "I don't think you said more than three words all night."

He shrugged but there was something in his eyes.

"What is it? What's going on?"

He flashed her a smile then but it looked forced and didn't touch his eyes. "Come on," he said, tugging her elbow. "Let's get to that party before Lucia starts to think we stood her up."

* * * *

The party was in full swing when they arrived. A dance club was hosting the after party and Lucia had left their names with the bouncer, as she'd promised. Lucia spotted them through the thick crowd and came over to greet them.

"Hey, you two. So glad you could make it."

Lucia was quickly waved over to a table of models, leaving Holly and Jack to fend for themselves. "My God," Holly said. "I've never seen so many beautiful women in one place." She looked over to Jack who was watching her. "This must be your idea of heaven." Jack smiled but yet again it looked forced. "Is everything all right?" she asked.

He nodded and took her by the hand to head toward the bar. "Come on, let's get some drinks."

Holly was keenly aware of the eyes that followed them as they made their way through the crowd. Somehow over the past few days it had become easy to forget that Jack was a celebrity. But now, in this crowd in particular, she caught every glance, every whisper…and every flash of photography. They reached the bar and she tugged her hand from his.

Maggie Dallen

"Is something wrong?" he asked.

"This place is crawling with photographers," she said, leaning in so he could hear her over the music.

"So?" Jack raised a hand to beckon the bartender and gave Holly a blank look. Really? Did she really have to spell it out for him? Apparently so.

"So, I don't want to end up in the gossip pages again," she said. She waited until he ordered and the bartender went off to get their drinks before she continued. "We agreed to end this little farce, remember?"

Jack's eyes burned into her and she shifted uncomfortably. When he spoke his voice was unusually hard. "Of course, we wouldn't want Benjamin getting the wrong impression."

Holly frowned at the nasty way he said Benjamin's name. "What?"

His normally rakish grin was more of a smirk as he leaned in. "Heaven forbid the almighty Benjie finds out we actually slept together."

Holly leaned in a little closer and got a heavy whiff of alcohol. She knew he'd been drinking more than usual at dinner but she hadn't known he was like this. "Are you drunk?"

He shrugged and took a giant sip of the straight whiskey he'd ordered. "Maybe."

His attention was nabbed by something over her right shoulder because he peered past her with a look of disgust before cursing a little too loudly. She smiled at the people nearby who looked over. *Nothing to see here, just a drunken celebrity who's in a foul mood, apparently.*

She turned to see what had made him curse and muttered an oath of her own under her breath. Robert and Miranda were heading their way. *Of course they were here.*

"Well, if it isn't the happy couple," Robert drawled as they drew near. Miranda gave her a rueful smile before kissing her cheek as her husband and Jack greeted one another with a barely civil nod.

"What are you doing here?" Jack asked. Holly swatted his arm and shot him a look but he ignored her.

"Miranda wouldn't miss it, she's a fan of the designer." If Robert or Miranda noted how rude Jack sounded, they didn't mention it. "What about you two?" Miranda asked. She turned to Holly, "Are you a fan as well?"

Holly shook her head, "Our friend is a fan. She invited us to tag along." While the women chatted, Robert and Jack stood in awkward silence. Holly looked over and realized that Jack was all but glaring at Robert.

"Is something wrong?" Robert asked.

Jack chugged the remainder of his whiskey and shook his head, his brown hair flopping into his eyes with the movement. "Nothing at all, my girlfriend here was just about to do me the honor of a dance."

He wrapped an arm around her and started to lead her onto the dance floor under the watchful eyes of the curious crowd. "What are you doing?" she hissed, trying to remove herself from his grasp.

Holly was excruciatingly aware of the cameras aimed in their direction as they headed to the dance floor. She saw people talking about them while they gawked. What were the odds this lovely couple moment wasn't going to be caught on film?

Jack pulled her into his arms and they began to move in time to the music. His body felt so good pressed against hers, his warm male scent made her want to ignore the stares. His hands on her back, pressing her against him made her wish she could forget everything and lose herself in the feel of him, and the insistent beat of the music.

But Benjamin's note was still her top priority. He was giving her another chance to prove that she wasn't a flake and she would be damned if she screwed it up. Heat flooded her cheeks but it had nothing to do with the eyes that were on them and everything to do with the man who was holding her close right now, leaning in as though he might....

"What are you doing?"

Jack paused momentarily, his eyes, glazed with drink fixed on hers for a moment. "I'm kissing you."

* * * *

She tasted like wine and strawberries. Her lips moved beneath his, despite her apparent anger. He didn't want to tear himself away but even in his state, he knew they were making a spectacle.

Grudgingly he pulled back, but he didn't release her from his arms. Jack knew he was being a jerk but he couldn't seem to help it. Reason had gone out the window ages ago and all he cared about now was holding onto the woman in his arms. The woman who was glaring up at him.

God, she was sexy when she was pissed. Did Benjamin appreciate that? Probably not. Hell, he'd probably never even seen her angry, and there was no chance he'd ever made her this mad. Nooo, not the sainted Benjamin.

She pulled back from him and tugged his hand, all but dragging him from the dance floor. One thing was certain. Holly was stronger than she looked.

Or he was drunker than he'd realized.

Either way, he was being dragged off the dance floor by a feisty blonde. When they reached an area near the bar with a modicum of privacy, she asked again. "What do you think you're doing?"

Hadn't he already answered that question?

"They're taking pictures," she continued, gesturing to the room at large. "We're going to be in the gossip pages again and I can't allow that. I told you that."

"Why not?" he asked. He knew why not but he wanted to hear her say it. The masochist in him needed to hear her say it.

Her eyes widened in disbelief. "Benjamin!" she said.

He winced. God, he really hated that name.

"He's giving me another chance," she continued. "Please don't screw this up for me."

That was it. Jack's patience had hit the limit. "You don't need another chance," he said. "You are perfect just the way you are." He watched her mouth drop open in shock and was dimly aware that his words were slightly slurred. Dammit, he really shouldn't have slammed that last drink.

But he had her attention now and it was suddenly imperative that he tell her. Everything. Reaching for her hands, he pulled her closer so he didn't have to yell over the music. "You are perfect," he said again, this time watching as her forehead creased in a quizzical look that was as adorable as it was heartbreaking. No one had told her this before. That was just wrong. This woman should hear those words every day of her life.

"Holly, you are the most amazing woman I've ever met. You're loyal and kind and funny and unpredictable." He swallowed the little voice of sobriety that was telling him to shut his mouth.

"Jack, what are you—" He cut her off with another kiss. When he pulled back her expression was stunned, dazed almost.

"You should be with someone who thinks you're amazing just the way you are." Her eyes met his and he drew in a deep breath. "You should be with me."

Despite the music that pulsed around them, Holly's silence was deafening. Jack's heart seemed to take a vacation from beating as he waited for her reaction. Instead, he heard Miranda's voice in his ear. "Here you are. You two looked great out there."

"Yeah, the center of attention, as usual," Robert added.

Their arrival, or maybe it was their words, seemed to snap Holly out of her stunned state. "I have to go," she said, pulling her hands out of his. "I have to get out of here."

He watched her get swallowed up in the crowd and felt his heart leave with her. What had he done?

* * * *

"What did you do?" Robert asked, his tone accusatory. Jack couldn't bring himself to get defensive, he just shook his head.

"Don't wanna talk about it," he slurred.

Miranda peered at him over her wine glass. "Jack, are you drunk?"

He didn't respond, he was too busy watching the spot where Holly had disappeared, hoping against hope to see her magically reappear.

She didn't.

It was Robert who finally got his attention. "What did you do to make her so angry, Jack?"

Jack was too busy staring at the Bermuda Triangle to turn and look at him but Robert continued on. "Let me guess. You did something selfish."

Jack was dimly aware of Miranda's voice trying to calm her husband and reassure Jack but Jack was through listening to his brother's criticisms. He'd just poured his heart out to a woman for the first time in his life—and she'd walked away. The alcohol was doing a decent job of numbing the pain but emotions were close to the surface and Robert's harsh words brought all of the old resentments back in a tidal wave.

"What do you want from me, Robbie?" He turned around so quickly, his brother and sister-and-law jerked back in surprise. "Seriously, what do you want? I paid back all the money I owed you, with interest."

His brother stared at him open-mouthed. His shock would have been funny if Jack was in a humorous sort of mood. But he wasn't. Far from it. Jaw clenched, he forced the words out slowly, enunciating every word. "How many times do I have to apologize?"

Miranda was staring at him with wide eyes and for a moment he thought she might cry, but she kept her composure. Robert's mouth snapped shut and he moved so he was mere inches in front of Jack. "Once," he said. "Just once."

Jack blinked in surprise. For a long moment, he and Robert stared at one another, years' worth of anger and resentment as solid as a brick wall between them. Jack's cloudy mind raced through memories of their interactions since their great fallout. Had he ever apologized? He knew he'd felt guilt but had he ever actually said the words? His stomach twisted in horror. No. He'd been too proud, too stupid, too…selfish.

"I'm sorry," he said. Those two words, so simple and so short, seemed to physically affect his brother.

For the first time in years, Robert smiled at him—a genuine, warm smile. "Was that so hard?" he asked. Jack shook his head. "I guess not."

There was an awkward silence in which Miranda beamed at the two men, who were suddenly and irrefutably uncomfortable. Jack had no idea what they were supposed to talk about now that years of tension was broken.

"So what did you do to piss off your girlfriend?" Robert asked. This time his tone was slightly less accusatory.

Jack heaved a sigh. His fuzzy brain thought of how to explain that one. Yeah, now was not the time. He would have plenty of time when he was sober to explain that little lie. For now, it seemed enough to say, "I blew it."

Yup, that about summed it up.

Jack saw Robert and Miranda exchange a knowing look. "Well there's only one thing for you to do," Miranda said.

Robert tapped his beer bottle against Jack's shoulder. "Make it right."

* * * *

Make it right. The words echoed in his brain long after he arrived back at the apartment many hours later. It was dark when he stumbled in and so quiet, Holly and Lucia must have been asleep. He'd left his brother and sister-in-law at the party and walked the whole, long way back to Brunelli's.

He'd replayed the scene with Holly and relived the stunned look in her eyes and how upset she'd looked when he'd kissed her in public, going against her wishes. She'd trusted him to help her win Benjamin back and he'd let her down. He'd been selfish, as usual, just like Robert had said.

Well it was time to make things right. Much as he might hate it, Holly had made her decision and had chosen the man she wanted to be with. And she'd made the right choice. Well, maybe not with Benjamin the wonder stud but in not choosing him. He'd told Holly right off the bat that he wasn't the type of guy she was looking for and he'd proven it time and time again. He couldn't be counted on to be a real boyfriend let alone a husband and father—and that's what Holly wanted. What she deserved.

Make it right. He knew what he had to do. He had to help Holly get everything she wanted and then he needed to walk away. He may be able to do the right thing but there was no way he would be able to sit by and watch her swoon over Benjamin. He was trying his best to be a good guy but he was no saint.

He flipped open his laptop and gave the orders that would put his plan into action. When he was done, he took a shower and threw on some fresh clothes. It was close to dawn and his limo back to the airport was probably already waiting for him. He hovered outside of Holly's door.

The urge to go in there and say goodbye was nearly overwhelming. He let his head drop against the closed door and his torturous mind imagined what she would look like all curled up beneath her covers, sound asleep. Who was he kidding? If he went in there now, the hounds of hell would have to drag him back out. It was hard enough leaving as it was.

Chapter 12

Holly sipped the café au lait her friend had kindly brought home for her and tried to ignore Lucia's puppy dog eyes.

"Now do you want to talk about it?"

"No." Ever since the two women had woken up this morning, later than usual, and found Jack's hastily scribbled note on the kitchen table, Lucia had been incessantly trying to get her to talk about what had transpired the night before.

Apparently Jack's very public embrace and her abrupt departure had caused quite a stir at the party. After a night of restless tossing and turning, Holly was no closer to figuring out what she was feeling about Jack's drunken confession, let alone what she was going to do about it. And then, when she'd come out here to find that Jack had left the apartment, without even saying goodbye, just a brief note saying he had to get back to work—her emotions had gone into overdrive and there was no making heads or tails of them. She was upset, ready to cry, and irritable.

Lucia pushed the bag of pastries across the table to her as a peace offering. "Okay, I won't ask again, I promise. But when you're ready to talk about it…" Holly nodded her head with a roll of her eyes.

"You'll be the first to know."

She reached over to grab a pastry. "So what about you?" she asked. "How was your night?"

Lucia's eyes lit up as she talked about the famous designers she'd talked to and the new styles she'd seen on the runway. Holly was only half paying attention—one part of her brain was having a hard time shutting off the movie reel of the night before—but she couldn't help but smile at her friend's enthusiasm.

"Lucia, if fashion means so much to you, why aren't you pursuing it as a career?"

Lucia's mouth clamped shut and a series of emotions crossed her face before she let out a sigh. "It's a long story. And I don't want to talk about me, I want to talk about you. I saw you and Jack last night. What did he say to you before you stormed out of there?"

Holly's cheeks grew warm at that description. She *had* made a rather dramatic exit. Lucia was watching her with wide, expectant eyes. What had Jack said to make her leave like that?

"He told me I was perfect."

The quiet words slipped out and Lucia stared at her in shocked silence for a moment before she whispered, "That bastard."

Holly choked on a laugh. "You don't understand, he…he…" He what? Told her she was perfect just the way she was. Her heart squeezed at the memory. *You should be with me.*

For a moment she struggled for breath, the memory of those words was so powerful. Jack wanted her. More than that, he thought she was perfect just the way she was. She allowed herself a moment to revel in those powerful, dizzying words before drawing herself back to reality.

Wake up, Holiday. Jack was drunk when he said that. He's made it abundantly clear that he's not looking for a girlfriend or commitments. And even if he was, he's not part of the plan.

Lucia was still waiting for her to explain why she'd run away after Jack's drunken confession. She took a deep, steadying breath. "Jack is great and we've been having a lot of fun together but I got an email from Benjamin yesterday and—"

Lucia cut her off with a loud groan. Holly watched her friend dramatically drop her head into her hands. When she looked up, her eyes were pleading. "When are you going to let go of that fantasy, Holly?"

Lucia's words were a punch in the gut. Her kneejerk reaction was to defend herself. She'd been doing it for nearly a year to her friends and family and the words came quick and vehement. "It's not a fantasy, it's a life plan. It's what I want."

Lucia was silent but the look in her eyes spoke volumes. It was pity. Her friend felt sorry for her. Anger warred with humiliation. She hated having to defend herself but for one brief moment she saw herself through her friend's eyes and she did seem pitiful. Like it wasn't bad enough that she'd tried to chase after him halfway around the world only to be rejected by him. Now, with one little hint of a chance together, she was dropping everything. Where was her pride?

You should be with someone who thinks you're amazing just the way you are. You should be with me.

Maggie Dallen

A lump formed in her throat making any more arguments impossible. Lucia leaned forward and placed her hand on top of Holly's. "Look, I'm not going to tell you who you should be with or what you should be looking for in life. Only you can figure that out. I'm just saying…" Holly found herself holding her breath waiting for her young friend to speak. A little part of her was hoping whatever she would say would wipe away the confusing muddled emotions that were making it impossible to think straight.

Lucia smiled at her. "I've got to catch a flight back to Italy this afternoon, which means you'll be on your own here until you're ready to join us at the villa."

Holly nodded. The idea of being alone with her thoughts was overwhelming.

Lucia seemed to read her mind. "There is no better place to figure out what's truly in your heart than Paris. All I'm saying is take your time to sort things out before you take the next step, okay?"

Holly gave a jerky nod. "You're probably right. A little alone time is just what I need."

"Speaking of." Lucia held up Jack's ridiculously short note. "Where do you think he went?"

Holly shrugged. "Probably back to Italy, I'd imagine." She tried to ignore the empty pit that had formed in her stomach the moment she'd realized he was gone. What had he been thinking when he'd written that? What had he been feeling? Was he hurt by her rejection or was his pride just wounded? Maybe he was just embarrassed. Or maybe he didn't even remember what he'd said. There was every possibility he regretted saying anything at all. He probably hadn't meant a word of it. Holly saw the look in his eyes when he was pouring his heart out. No, he'd meant it. Or at least, he'd meant it in that moment. Who knows how he'd felt in the cold light of day.

One question had been repeating itself over and over all morning. Why hadn't he said goodbye?

* * * *

Jack was trying his best to ignore Daniel's questions but despite his best efforts, he couldn't get his business partner to talk about business.

"So you just…left?" Daniel asked for the millionth time.

"Yes, Danny, I left. Now can we please look at that spreadsheet your assistant sent over?" Jack was just as surprised as Daniel that he was the one who was opting to talk business rather than romance but after the night he'd had, the last thing he wanted to do was focus on Holly.

Daniel, on the other hand, was obsessed. "Did you tell her you love her?"

Jack's hand froze while reaching for his iced tea. *Love.* There it was. The word that had been taunting him ever since he sobered up and could face the fact that he had temporarily lost his mind. Was it because he was in love? He'd seen plenty of friends—namely Daniel and Ivy—turn into complete idiots in the name of the L-word but he'd never experienced it himself.

But yeah, he supposed that was the only explanation for the complete and utter havoc that Holly's presence in his life had wrought. *Wonderful.* He'd finally gone and fallen in love and it was with a woman who loved someone else.

He'd always been a screw-up but this was taking things to an entirely new level. He'd gone and messed up everything. Not only was she the only woman he ever wanted to be with, she was also always going to be in his life. Forever. She would always be his best friend's sister and unless he wanted to cut all ties with Ivy and break up a perfectly wonderful business partnership with Daniel, Holly would be in his life.

That thought was simultaneously a searing pain and a soothing balm.

He hadn't lost her forever. She would be around...just not his. But he could still talk to her, laugh with her...maybe give her a quick hug on occasion.

Okay, yeah, that would be too painful for words. Best to stick with the occasional chitchat at major life events like baptisms and birthdays. He could handle that. One day maybe he'd even find a way not to openly despise Benjamin.

"Jack." Daniel's sharp voice cut through his runaway train of thoughts and he looked up to see Daniel's hard stare fixed on him.

"What?"

"Did you tell her that you love her?" Daniel repeated the words slowly as though talking to a dim-witted child.

"No," Jack said. The words were hard to get out of his throat.

Daniel sighed and ran a hand through his hair. "Then you are an idiot."

Jack stared at his friend in surprise. "Excuse me?"

Daniel was shaking his head in disappointment. "You're a coward if you don't fight for her. Hell, if Ivy hadn't fought for me I might still be sitting here alone and miserable."

"But she doesn't want me, she wants Benjamin."

Daniel's look could only be described as pitying. "And before I met Ivy, I thought I wanted a life of solitude—a life of business deals and meaningless affairs. Sometimes people don't know what they want until it's right in front of their faces."

* * * *

Holly spent the day doing all of the things she loved in Paris. She went to museums, she stopped into cafes, she did some window shopping... and she was miserable. The more she tried to sort through the jumble of emotions and thoughts, the more confused she became. The only thing she knew for certain was that she wished Jack was with her.

She missed his jokes, his laughter, the way he listened without judgment, his reassuring touches, his kisses... Paris just wasn't the same without him. She thought about calling him, seeing where he was and what he was doing but she stopped herself every time. He'd left. Clearly he didn't want to see her or talk about the things he'd said the night before. For all she knew, he regretted every word.

She tried to focus on Benjamin. She should be happy right now, she should be celebrating the fact that Benjamin was willing to give them a shot. Maybe. Well, he wasn't ruling them out. Somehow that just wasn't enough to make her dance for joy.

She needed to talk to Jack and clear the air at the very least. After an exhausting and unproductive day of wallowing she returned to Brunelli's apartment but the luxurious apartment just felt...big. Too big for one person.

A knock on the door interrupted her packing. Jack! He was back. She knew he wouldn't leave things like that. She all but ran to the door and threw it open.

"Hey, Holiday. Miss me?" Benjamin grinned at her in the hallway and Holly's heart fell. She swallowed thick tears of disappointment that it wasn't Jack on the other side of that door.

She tried to shove aside the disappointment. She was just in shock, that was all. How had he found her? What was he doing at Brunelli's? Of course she was ecstatic to see Benjamin. She should be over the moon. She was just...confused, that was all.

Benjamin raised his brows in a questioning look. "Uh, can I come in?"

"Oh, yes, of course, come on in," she said, ushering him inside and showing him where to leave his luggage. The whole time her brain was going a million miles an hour trying to figure out what he was doing there and, more importantly, what his sudden appearance meant.

Once he was settled, she led him to the balcony where the sunset was washing the city in an orange glow.

Benjamin whistled. "This is one amazing view."

"Mmm," she said. He settled in beside her and they sat in silence for a moment before she finally asked the question. "Benjamin...what are you doing here? I mean, don't get me wrong, it's great to see you but...."

"But I'm not the type to hop on a plane on a whim?" he finished.

"Exactly," she said with a laugh. "So, what's up?"

Benjamin wiped his hands across his jeans in an unusual show of nerves. "Well, Holiday, I guess you and me have got a lot to talk about."

This was it. There was no way Benjamin flew all this way to let her down easy. She waited for the swell of excitement, the butterflies in her stomach, the trembling limbs. Instead her mouth went dry and her stomach did a twist before flopping low in her belly.

Benjamin looked over her shoulder at the view for a moment before speaking. "The thing is, Holly, I'm worried about you."

Holly's head jerked back. That was so not the declaration of love she'd been waiting for. "Excuse me?"

"I'm worried," he said again. "We all are—your parents, your sister, my family."

Holly struggled to draw in breath. "So you all have been talking about me?"

Benjamin's face was creased with concern. "Not in a bad way, Holiday. We're just...."

"Worried, yeah I got that."

She shook her head and brushed aside a hand that he reached out to squeeze her shoulder in a brotherly fashion. "I can't believe this,"

"What?" Honest confusion clouded his eyes. Could he really not understand?

"I thought you were here for..." she left off with a sigh and tried again. "When you showed up like that I thought it was because you'd decided you wanted to...be with me." She had to force the words out between stiff lips.

This wasn't romantic—hell, it wasn't even kind, it was...annoying.

Benjamin's expression had gone from mild confusion to sympathetic understanding and that was so much worse. His sympathy was dangerously close to pity. "Holiday, I meant what I said. I think we *might* have a future together, I just don't want to rush into anything."

Holly shut her eyes and fought the impulse to cover her ears. That's exactly what he'd said in the email. She'd thought he was just being cautious—Benjamin was nothing if not prudent. But there was caution and then there was cowardice and she couldn't stand the latter.

"It's not that complicated Benjamin. Do you want to be with me or don't you?"

Now it was his turn to jerk back as though she'd just struck him. She watched his eyes widen in surprise at the simple question.

"I guess…I don't know, I guess I always thought we would get together, you know? Eventually?"

She nodded. Oh, she knew.

"But, whenever I've tried to picture what our life would be like…I just can't see it," he said the words with such sadness, it was almost funny. Almost. But then he turned to her with an intensity that was unnerving, particularly coming from this particular laid-back, non-confrontational man.

"What about you?" he demanded. "What do you see when you picture our future together?"

She opened her mouth but no words could come out. She tried to conjure up the image of their future marriage and children but nothing was coming. Her mind had gone blank. He didn't wait long before he continued on. "Because every time you talk about your future in Oakdale," he started and then shook his head as though words couldn't express his frustration.

"What?" Holly asked. "Every time I talk about it…what?"

He let out a loud exhale. "Every time you talk about your future it sounds like you're describing an episode of *Little House on the Prairie*."

Holly gasped at that and then found herself staring at Benjamin in shocked silence until they both were fighting back snickering laughs. "Really?" she asked, losing the battle with laughter as Benjamin joined her.

"Really," he said.

She tilted her head to the side as she thought about the fantasy she'd become so focused on. She pictured the house, the white picket fence, the adorable little children running in the yard, the dog barking in the yard. Her eyes widened in horror. She was allergic to dogs.

He was right. She had created a lovely, one-dimensional, *completely delusional* fantasy world. She turned to stare out at the view and shot Benjamin a sideways look. "Okay, fine. Maybe you're right. Maybe it's not entirely based on reality."

Benjamin's smile was soft and kind and so reassuring. That was what she'd always been drawn to—the comfortable, reliable, and oh-so-dependable friend. He reached out and grabbed her hand and a little part of Holly's brain was aware of the fact that there was no electric spark at the touch of his skin, no pulsing energy between them to make the air thicken with sexual tension. There was just…friendship.

"Look, Holiday, I'm not saying there's no possibility of a future for us, I'm just saying…."

She stopped him by putting a hand on his arm. "Hey, I get it. I do." Also, she was fairly certain she would scream if she heard him say, "I don't want to rush into anything" one more time.

He nodded then and they both turned to watch the sun sink below the skyline. "So, if you didn't come here to win me over," she finally said. "Why did you come?"

He looked to her in surprise. "I told you, I was—"

"Worried, yeah I know. But you shouldn't have spent all that money just to come talk some sense into me."

His eyes were crinkled in confusion as he watched her. "I didn't spend any money," he said, as though this was something obvious she should have known.

"What do you mean? How did you get here?"

He pulled back then and a slow smile spread across his face as though he just discovered a secret. "He didn't tell you?" Benjamin asked.

A buzzing sound filled her head for a moment and she knew what Benjamin was going to say before he said it. "Your friend sent me the plane ticket. He said you needed to see me."

Holly licked her dry lips. "My friend?" Her voice sounded far away.

"Yeah, Jack. Hey, are you all right?"

Holly reached out a hand to clutch the railing and steady herself. Jack had sent Benjamin to her. Tears stung the back of her eyes as the full weight of that news hit her straight in the heart.

But what did it mean? He'd sent her the man she'd said she wanted. Was he feeling guilty about the things he'd said or did he not mean them at all? Either way, sending Benjamin was the least selfish thing she'd ever seen.

The need to see Jack was so overwhelming she almost ran away but she had no idea where he was. Was he even in Paris anymore?

Benjamin was watching her with narrowed eyes. "What's going on?"

She shook her head. She wished she knew. Did this gesture mean he was giving up or that he cared more about her and what she wanted than he did about himself? Her mind flashed back to the look on Jack's face when he'd told her he couldn't be with her, that he could never give her what she wanted.

He was an idiot.

She thought of the way he'd been there for her; the way he'd listened and cared and never asked for anything in return. That was the guy he was. All that talk of being unable to commit was just regurgitated crap that he'd come to believe. He had changed. Sometime over the course of his adult life Jack had become a reliable, kind and generous man. But he couldn't see it. He couldn't see the kind of future he could have if he just trusted himself.

And her.

Her breath left her lungs in a rush of air as her heart beat into double time. Images of the life they could have together raced through her mind. And these weren't static pictures off the cover of a Hallmark card like they had been with Benjamin. These were real. She could see them laughing and traveling and having new experiences together. She could see them as a family. Unconventional, sure, but who wanted conventional? Not her. These new fantasies…they felt solid…they felt like her.

That was a life she wanted. A life of shared respect and mutual admiration. A life where they grew together. A life built on trust and friendship and…love.

"Holly, are you okay?" Benjamin asked. He was leaning toward her, his brows drawn together in concern.

Was she all right? She wasn't sure. The world had momentarily flipped upside down before righting itself with a start. Or at least that's how it felt. Her brain was reeling as it tried to keep up with her heart, which ached with unspoken emotions.

She needed to see him. She needed to make things right.

"I have to find Jack," she whispered. "I think…I think I love him."

The word felt strange on her tongue, like she was learning a new language.

Benjamin's grin was so comforting, she nearly wept. "I think he probably feels the same way."

Holly winced at the memory of her last words to him. Of the look on his face when she'd walked away. "I'm not so sure."

"Well, all I know is, flying me all the way out here is a pretty grand gesture for someone who doesn't care."

Holly's heartrate picked up speed at that. "You think so?"

His grin was answer enough. "How can I help?"

Ivy shook her head. "You can't. This one I have to do on my own." She reached out a hand and he took it. She struggled to find the right words to explain what she was feeling. Her best friend had flown all the way to France to save her, after all. "You are always coming to my rescue," she said. "Ever since we were kids. And I love that about you. I love that you're always there when I need you. But I think...I think maybe Jack needs *me*. I want to be the one who comes to the rescue this time. Does that make sense?"

He nodded. "It does. And you know what? Maybe it's time I find someone who lights up at the sight of me like you just did over Jack." He was teasing her, but he was right. He deserved to be with someone who was truly in love with him and didn't just see him as reliable or comfortable.

"So what now?" Benjamin asked.

Holly sighed. "I'm going to Italy."

Chapter 13

Traffic was at a crawl as Holly tried to make her way out of the city. Her stomach was a jumble of knots as she tried to figure out what he would say once she saw Jack. There was every possibility he was regretting the things he'd said the night before.

There was every chance he was still convinced he couldn't be in a real relationship. The sting of that rejection still hurt. He was wrong, she knew he was. Jack had a bigger heart than anyone she knew. The only thing keeping him from making a real commitment was his misguided belief that he wasn't capable. His brother had done a brilliant job undermining Jack's confidence and making him believe that he was selfish and unreliable.

Her fingers clenched her purse which sat on her lap in the backseat of the taxi. She wished she could give Robert a piece of her mind. No sooner had the thought crossed her mind than she recognized the neighborhood surrounding her. They were very close to Robert and Miranda's apartment. "Can you stop here please?" she said.

Miranda opened on the first knock. She ignored Miranda's wide-eyed look of surprise. "Is Robert here?"

Miranda ushered her in and led her into the living room where Robert sat reading a book.

"Holly, it's nice to see you—"

Holly cut him off with a wave of her hand. She had no desire to exchange niceties with this man who kept meddling in her love life. She was here to give him a piece of her mind and that was exactly what she would do.

"Listen up," she started, causing both Robert and Miranda to stare at her in surprise. "You are so incredibly blind when it comes to your brother, it's not even funny."

"Excuse me?" Robert started.

"No, I don't excuse you," Holly said. "You have been underestimating and misjudging your brother for years and thanks to you, he is under this incredibly stupid delusion that he can't be in a serious relationship."

Her voice had risen a bit despite her best intentions to remain calm. She was dimly aware that Miranda had picked up her phone and was dialing. Probably calling security to have her kicked out of their apartment. She'd better be quick.

Taking a deep breath, she started in again, "I may not know everything that went down between the two of you but I know this—Jack is smart, caring, kind, and generous to a fault. He is so incredibly selfless, it's…" A lump in her throat cut her short. The fact that Jack had sent Benjamin to her…she still didn't know what to make of it. She didn't know if she should be touched by the thoughtfulness of the gesture or pissed that he was giving up on her so easily. Or maybe he didn't care as much as she hoped? She shoved that thought to the side. She would confront Jack soon enough and make him see what they had together. But right now she had two very bewildered Everetts standing before her and she had to finish what she'd come to say.

Clearing her throat, she continued. "I know he's made mistakes over the years but you know what? That's called being human. And the fact that you can't bring yourself to forgive him is…well, frankly it's just stupid."

She saw Miranda fighting back laughter as she held the phone up so security could hear her tirade. Oh hell, she was giving some doorman a good show at least. It was probably a matter of minutes before she was thrown out of here.

"You have been too blinded by anger and, let's face it, probably jealousy, to realize that Jack has grown up. He's changed. If you bothered to get to know Jack now, as an adult, you'd see that he risked throwing away a major fortune for my sister, out of loyalty and friendship. You'd see that he works his butt off every single day to make sure his company is a success. If you paid attention you'd see that your brother is the most committed, reliable, loving man you know."

Robert's jaw was somewhere near the ground by the time she came to an end. The silence in the room was deafening. When neither of her audience members responded, she picked up her purse where she'd thrown it on the couch and edged toward the front door. "Okay, well, that's uh—that's all I came to say. Um….have a good night."

* * * *

Jack was just as speechless as his brother and sister-in-law on the other end of the phone. When Brunelli found him on the veranda a little while later, he was still clutching the phone and staring into space trying to digest all that he'd heard.

Holly had stood up for him. To his brother. Everything she'd said... she'd sounded so certain, so passionate. It was an odd feeling seeing oneself from someone else's point of view. Normally when he did it was from the point of view of his brother or his parents...or the press. But the way Holly saw him—she saw the best in him, the man he wanted to be. The man he was trying to become. The tightness in his chest was so painful he pressed a hand to his heart tried to draw in a deep breath.

"You're too young to have a heart attack," Brunelli said as he walked toward him. "Leave that to me."

He plopped down in the seat beside Jack with a grin but his smile faded quickly as he watched him. "What's going on? Is something wrong?"

Jack forced the words out. "I'm an idiot."

At that Brunelli tossed his head back with a laugh. "Tell me something I don't know."

They both turned at the sound of the villa's back door opening behind them. Ivy marched out with Daniel close behind. "Jack Everett, you are an idiot," Ivy called.

Daniel was following right behind him and looked like he was torn between laughter and concern. "Honey, please calm down."

Jack glared at Daniel over Ivy's shoulder. "You told her?"

Daniel shrugged, amusement apparently winning out. "Sorry, Jack, she's ruthless when it comes to her family."

"Why didn't you tell me you like Holly?" she demanded. She'd come to a stop directly in front of him with her hands on her hips.

"Umm." He turned to Brunelli for help but the old man was watching him with an expectant grin that said he was enjoying the younger man's awkward situation. He shifted in his chair and glanced away but when he looked back Ivy was still glaring at him.

"I didn't think you'd approve," he said.

Her eyes grew so big he drew back in alarm. "Are you kidding me? You are one of my favorite people in the world, Jack Everett, why on earth would I not want you with my sister?"

He opened his mouth to speak but drew a blank. Where to begin? Because he was a notorious playboy? Because he had a lifetime of screw-ups under his belt? Because he'd never been in a long-term relationship before?

Because he'd never been in love before.

Jack dropped his head into his hand.

When he looked up again it was to see all three watching him with obvious concern. "I don't know what to do."

"Does she feel the same way?" Ivy asked.

Jack shrugged. "No, I don't think so. I mean, she loves Benjamin—"

"Oh please," Ivy said with a wave of her hand. "Holly is deluding herself into thinking they would be a good match but anyone who has seen the two of them together knows that they are not in love."

Some of the tightness in his chest eased a bit at that proclamation. But even if she didn't love Benjamin, that didn't mean she loved him. He thought of the speech he'd just heard her give. Those were some strong feelings he'd heard in her voice. Maybe, just maybe, he had a chance. Or maybe he was reading too much into it, maybe she loved him as a friend.

He couldn't stop the groan of misery that slipped out.

Ivy sat in the seat beside him and grabbed his hand. When she spoke it was to her husband who was hovering nearby. "Why are people in love so stupid?"

Jack nearly groaned aloud again. Was it that obvious? Daniel just shook his head. "What we need to do is come up with a plan."

Brunelli was nodding his head in agreement and Ivy's eyes lit up in excitement. Jack's tone was wary when he finally spoke, "What kind of plan? How do you expect me to fix things with Holly when I've made a mess of things since the first moment I met her?"

He told them about the wedding—about how he'd had the most amazing night of his life…and then walked away from her.

"Yes, but she walked away from you too." Ivy pointed out with a nonchalant shrug. "The way I see it, you were both idiots."

"Okay, fine. But then I went and—"

"Saved her from herself by tracking her down in Paris?" Daniel finished. "I'd think most women would find that quite gallant." He looked to his wife for confirmation and she gave them both an eager nod.

"But then I dragged her into my family drama," Jack said. "She saw me at my absolute worst."

"And she stood up for you," Brunelli pointed out. "From what you told us, it sounds like you've found the perfect match. A woman who understands where you've come from and sees you for who you truly are today."

"A good man," Daniel said. "A responsible business partner and a loyal friend."

"A reliable, generous, and caring man," Ivy added. She had tears in her eyes but that was nothing new these days.

Jack was touched by their kind words more than he wanted to admit. His tone was gruff when he said, "Thanks, guys. I don't know if I'm the kind of man Holly deserves yet but being around her....she makes me want to be that guy."

Brunelli was giving him a fatherly grin of approval. "Finding someone who sees the best in you and who makes you want to be a better person... there is no better love than that."

Jack knew they were right. He'd found the one. The One. And he'd been too stupid to see it. He wiped a hand over his face as the full weight of his actions hit him.

"Okay, let's get started with a plan," Daniel said, in true Daniel style. The man lived for plans.

"It's too late," Jack said. He looked up to see them staring at him in confusion. "It's too late," he repeated. "I, uh, I flew Benjamin out to Paris...Paris, France. The two of them are probably planning out their future children's names by now."

He watched all three of their faces fall. "Well that was nice, I suppose," Ivy admitted. "But stupid."

Brunelli and Daniel murmured their agreement on his stupidity. It was official.

Brunelli looked lost in thought. "If you could, how would you make things right?"

Jack's laugh was humorless. "I would start over again. I would go back to Daniel and Ivy's wedding and do it right. I would sweep her off her feet and show her the kind of love she deserves. And once I had her in my arms, I would never let go."

The tears were streaming down Ivy's face by that point and Daniel was rubbing her back in consolation. "Well then that's just what we'll have to do," he said. The grim look on his face was simultaneously frightening and heartening. Daniel had a plan.

Brunelli apparently could read his mind because he and Daniel shared a look and the old man clapped his hands together in excitement. "I've got to find Lucia and the other grandkids. We have a lot of work to do."

Ivy and Jack were watching him walk away in confusion when Daniel turned to his wife. "Sweetheart, our baby is going to make an early appearance."

* * * *

Holly was already at the airport waiting standby for a seat to open up on the next flight to Italy when the call came.

"Daniel, is everything okay?"

"The baby is on the way." Holly barely heard him speak after that. She rushed to tell him, "I'm on my way" before he hung up the phone.

She looked around the airport with a smile. What excellent timing.

Having grabbed a seat on the next flight out, she arrived in Italy within hours and she spotted Lucia waiting for her near baggage claim.

"You got here quick," Lucia said after giving her a hug.

"Yeah, well, I was actually already on my way."

Lucia raised her brows in question. "Really? Why? I thought Benjamin had arrived in Paris. Wasn't that what you wanted?" Holly let out a sigh of annoyance at her own stupidity. "Yeah, well, I thought that's what I wanted but…I was wrong."

Lucia was smiling at her. "So what is it that you want? Or should I say who?"

Holly returned her grin and tried to ignore the nerves there wreaking havoc on her stomach. She wasn't sure she was ready to spill her guts just yet. Not when there was every chance that Jack could still reject her. His words from the night before had been haunting her all day.

Maybe she would never make him see reason. Or maybe he didn't love her. She swallowed down the doubts and insecurities as best she could. She would have her say and hope that she wasn't totally off base about their connection. She didn't think she could face the heartbreak if she was wrong.

But first thing's first, she had to be there for her sister and then she would worry about how to convince Jack that he was in love with her.

"Are we going to the hospital?" she asked. "Are my parents on their way?"

Lucia's smile was secretive. "Danny asked that you wait for him at the villa. I'll take you to the hospital when they're ready for visitors."

Holly nodded and focused on the view outside the window. She drew in a deep steadying breath. They were going to the villa. Would Jack be there? If so, what would she say? She wasn't ready. She wiped suddenly sweaty palms on her jeans and gnawed on her lower lip. She had to come up with a way to convince this man that she was worth taking a risk on. That he was capable of committing and that they were more than a casual fling.

Right. No pressure.

The house looked dark when they pulled up. "Where is everyone?" she asked.

Lucia shrugged and rushed ahead of her. "I'll ask one of the boys to come grab your bags. Why don't you go out on the veranda to wait, I'll be right out with something to eat."

Before she could protest or ask questions, Lucia had disappeared into the house and Holly followed the path on the side of the house that led to the veranda. The last time she'd been here was for Ivy's wedding. The night she'd met Jack.

The night her world had turned upside down.

She turned the corner of the house and gasped at the sight before her. Blinking rapidly, for one brief moment she thought perhaps she'd fallen and hit her head. There was no way this was reality.

It was the same. It was *exactly* the same. From the twinkling lights strung overhead to the outdoor stage with a ten-piece band—the veranda looked like Ivy and Daniel's wedding had just come to an end.

The music floated over to her softly and she looked around in wonder. A movement to her left caught her eye. He was silhouetted by the stage lights but she knew it was him.

"Jack," she said, her breath catching in her throat. Her brain was struggling to make sense of what was going on but her heart had leapt far ahead of her mind. Her heart tightened and her breathing came in ragged gasps as tears started to trickle down her cheeks.

He had done this. For her. That was the only explanation.

He reached her side and she could see his expression. His normally floppy hair was slicked back off of his face as it had been that night. He was wearing a tuxedo and he looked oh-so-amazing. He looked like a movie star. Too good to be true.

The only thing different was the look in his eyes. At the wedding he had been lighthearted, charming, filled with laughter and teasing. But now, she could swear she saw...fear.

"What is this?" she whispered.

Instead of replying, he held out a hand. "May I have this dance?"

She stepped into his arms and let him lead her in a waltz around the empty dance floor.

"You look beautiful," he said, his eyes melting her with their passion and their heat.

Blood rushed to her cheeks and she glanced down at her faded T-shirt and jeans with a laugh. "If I'd known this was a formal occasion...wait, Jack, where's Ivy, is she..."

"I'd imagined she's tucked into bed beside Daniel at the moment," Jack said, that familiar mischievous twinkle returning to his eyes as he explained. "I needed to see you. We figured the baby's arrival would get you here."

Holly choked on laughter and tears. "You know, that wasn't necessary. I was already on my way."

Jack stopped dancing, his eyes wide with surprise. "You were? Why?"

Holly shook her head. She wasn't ready to bare her soul yet, she had too many questions. "You first. Why go to all this trouble? What is this about?"

She thought she knew—she *hoped* she knew. But she needed to hear him say it.

"I wanted a do-over," Jack said. She saw a hint of that familiar lopsided grin as he gave her a rueful look. "I've been such an idiot, Holly. I should have done it all differently, from the first moment I met you."

The tears that had been threatening to fall trickled down her cheek. With the lights and the music…it was too much to take in. "What are you saying?" she asked.

He paused then and she saw fear war with conviction. "I love you," he said, the words coming out on a rush of air. "I think I loved you the moment I set eyes on you and if I'm being honest I was already head over heels crazy in love by the time we finished our first dance."

Holly's voice came out wobbly and soft. "You were?"

He nodded and the love she saw in his eyes at that moment was so heady she thought she might faint. She gripped his hand tighter and clung to his shoulder. "Why didn't you…do something or say something?"

He shook his head. "Because I didn't think I deserved you. I didn't think I had what it took to be the kind of man you needed."

"But now?" she asked.

He pulled her tighter against him and she could feel the rapid rise and fall of his chest as his arms crushed her to him. "Now I know that I would do anything to become the man you deserve. You make me want to be that man."

Holly beamed up at him, basking in the glow of his words and the feel of him beneath her arms. When he pulled away slightly, she clung to him even tighter. "What about you?" he asked. "I thought by now you and Benjamin would be—"

She cut him off with a quick shake of her head. "You were right," she admitted. Then with a little laugh she said, "Everybody was right. He's not the man for me. I guess I wanted…."

Jack nodded and to her amazement he understood. He got her in a way no one else could. She said the words anyway, more because she needed to say them more than he needed to hear them. "I thought I needed to be different in order to have the things that I want in life. Stability, family, commitment." He nodded and ran a hand through her curls sending a shiver down her spine. "I guess I didn't trust myself. Or trust that I could be enough just the way I am."

"And now?" Jack asked.

Holly felt a smile of contentment spread across her face. "Now I know that I can have it all, on my terms, in my way." She took a deep breath. "With you."

She saw the nervous tension break as he slumped forward so his forehead rested against hers. "Thank God," he whispered. "You have no idea how much I want to be that for you. I want it all with you."

"What are you saying, Jack?"

He moved so quickly that he twirled her with a flourish before pulling her back into his arms. They were both laughing and grinning like fools when he answered. "I'm saying...Miss Holly Sinclair, will you be my girlfriend?"

Gravity seemed to take a holiday for one breathless moment and Holly was certain Jack's arms were the only thing keeping her on the ground. "Yes," she started, her voice coming out breathless with sheer joy. "I would love to be your—"

The rest of her sentence was cut short as Jack pulled her in for a kiss to seal the deal.

When at last they came up for air, Holly wrapped her arms around Jack's neck and let her head drop against his shoulder.

"So what now?" His breath against her ear made her shiver.

Holly shrugged. "No idea." Tilting her head back, she met his gaze and her stomach did a little backflip at the raw emotions she saw there—the tenderness and the desire...and the love.

Jack dropped a light kiss on her lips and began moving her in time with the music. "You're an excellent dancer, did you know that?" He gave a wistful sigh. "I never should have let you go that night."

Laughter bubbled up at his melodramatic tone. "I'm here now."

Jack grinned and he dipped his head so his forehead rested lightly against her. "And I am never letting go."

As they danced beneath the twinkling terrace lights to the same music they'd listened to on that wedding night that felt so long ago, Holly giggled.

"What's so funny?" Jack asked, brushing a wayward curl out of her face.

"It's just..." Holly started. "You have this way of making me feel like Cinderella."

Jack lifted one brow. "Is that a bad thing?"

Holly laughed. "It's a great thing. But it's...."

"Not reality," Jack finished. "It's not a five-year goal or a life plan or any of those other boring things you seem so obsessed with lately."

Holly clamped her lips shut to keep from laughing at his teasing tone. For someone who was so in love with adventure, she *had* gone a bit overboard with the whole "stability" plan. Pulling him in closer, she said, "Maybe we should ease into this whole responsibility thing."

He flashed her that lopsided grin she could never resist. "I do have a plan, you know. It may not include white picket fences but I think it's a good start."

"What's that?" she asked.

"Whatever we do next, let's do it together."

Holly's heart leapt into overdrive as his lips claimed hers once again. She pulled back just long enough to say, "Deal."

Epilogue

"We don't have to do this, you know," Holly said.

Jack glanced up from the papers he had been about to sign to see Holly nibbling at her lower lip. Her eyes were wide and filled with nervous excitement. He knew that look. It was the same expression she'd worn right before they'd gone bungee jumping in Brazil.

Jack leaned over to plant a kiss on her lips and hopefully ease some of her anxiety. "We're doing this," he said. "It's about time you and I had a place of our own to call home."

Ivy walked out onto Brunelli's veranda holding her three-month-old little girl, followed closely by Daniel. These days it seemed Daniel was attached to his daughter by an invisible leash. Ivy took one look at the paper Jack was holding and let out an exasperated sigh.

"Don't tell me you two are still debating signing that lease."

"It's a big decision," Holly argued, reaching out to take her niece.

It *had* been a big decision. Not *if* they would rent a place together but where. There had been Oakdale, to be near Holly's parents, Italy to be close to his business partner or New York City, which Daniel and Ivy would be calling home now that baby Anna had arrived. They ended up opting for Paris so Jack could work on repairing his relationship with his brother. He and his family had a lot of time to make up for.

"But you're not even buying, you're just renting," Daniel said, sounding perplexed.

Jack caught Holly's eye and they shared a grin. They couldn't expect Daniel and Ivy to understand. He and Holly had been inseparable since the moment she agreed to be his girlfriend but now...now they would have a home together. It was a big step.

Holly gave him a wink and he reached out to take her free hand in his.

He turned back to sign the paper but was interrupted by Brunelli's arrival. The older man looked worried as he sat beside them at the table and reached out for his chance to hold the ever-in-demand newborn.

"Brunelli, what's wrong?" Holly asked.

"It's Lucia. She ran away."

Jack exchanged worried glances with Holly, Ivy, and Daniel. They'd all noticed that she hadn't been herself lately.

"What do you mean, 'ran away'?" he asked. "What about her fiancé? Did she and Marco elope?"

Brunelli tossed a note onto the table. "Read it for yourself. She says the wedding is off and she has gone to America."

They sat in stunned silence for a moment, taking in the news.

"Poor Lucia," Holly said.

Jack squeezed her hand.

Daniel reached out and picked up the note. "Gone to America," he read out loud. He shared a look with Jack. It was awfully vague for such a large country.

"She could be anywhere," Brunelli said. "She's just like her mother—willful and headstrong."

"Don't worry, Jack and I will find her. We'll make sure she's all right," Holly said.

Jack looked over at his girlfriend in surprise but when she turned to him with a questioning look, he nodded his agreement. Of course they would go after their friend.

Brunelli's anxiety seemed to subside a bit. "I know she's a grown woman and she can do what she likes but she's still my granddaughter."

Ivy patted his knee when he added, "Just like her mother," under his breath.

Once the others returned back to the house to put Baby Anna down for a nap, Jack turned to Holly, his eyes narrowed in suspicion. "Did you offer us up for the manhunt as a way to put off moving in with me?" he teased.

Holly's jaw dropped in mock offense. "I would never! We're obviously the most qualified couple for the job. I mean, do you really see Ivy and Daniel traipsing around the states looking for a runaway fashion designer? With a newborn in tow?"

Jack tapped his jaw and pretended to mull it over. "You have a point."

Holly wrapped her arms around his neck and pulled him close. "Maybe you're the one with cold feet now that we're settling down."

Maggie Dallen

Jack grinned and pulled her even closer. "I thought we agreed, no one here was 'settling'. But we *can* have a home together..." he trailed off, opting to drop kisses along her neck. Words were just not cutting it.

"Mmm," Holly sighed. Her head dropped back, giving him better access. "We don't need to sign a lease for that. My home is right here."

He pulled back just enough so he could look into her eyes. "That was very wise."

"I thought so." She flashed him an impish grin that made him laugh out loud.

He turned to the table and picked up the lease that had been lying there waiting for his signature. He waited to feel some sort of fight or flight instinct, some panicky remnant of a lifetime of commitment phobia. But all he felt was an undeniable excitement for the future. A future with this woman—his girlfriend, his future...his home.

Keep reading for sneak peek of book three of Maggie Dallen's A Chance Romance series!

Accidental Elopement

Available November 2016.

Learn more about Maggie Dallen at
http://www.kensingtonbooks.com/author.aspx/31712

**Accidental Engagement is now available at
www.kensingtonbooks.com**

Chapter 1

Lucia had exactly nine dollars and thirty-six cents in her pocket as she fought her way onto the crowded F-train heading downtown. Enough to buy one more coffee and a bagel—a combo she'd come to adore during her six-week stint in New York—but not much else.

She reached through a thick crowd of people so she could hold onto the cold metal pole in the middle of the train to keep her balance. *The subway.* That was one thing she would not miss when she left. But even that bit of optimism was enough to bring tears to her eyes. Who was she kidding? She was going to miss everything about this city, even the crowded, smelly subway.

She had just enough left on her Metrocard for a train to the airport but her credit card had long since maxed out and she had no clue how she could pay for the airfare.

You could call Grandpa.

She shook her head in disgust. It was bad enough that she was going back to Italy with her tail between her legs, there was no way she would beg her grandfather for the airfare home. When her grandmother was alive, she used to describe him as overprotective. More like smothering. Of course he only had her best interests at heart—as did her ex-fiancé—but that didn't mean they knew what was best. *She* would be the one to pave her future, even if it meant she failed.

Lucia watched as the subway door opened and closed before continuing on downtown. The next stop was SoHo. She knew where she had to go. If she was being honest with herself, she'd known where she was heading the moment she'd walked away from her disappointing meeting with her former boss—her last lifeline to the new life she'd been working for this past month.

Stifling a heavy sigh, she shifted to make room for another passenger who needed access to the pole. An older Hispanic man who was sitting on one of the orange plastic seats made a gesture, silently asking if she'd like his seat. She forced a smile and shook her head. "No thank you, I'm getting off at the next stop."

Daniel's hotel loomed taller than any other building in the trendy downtown neighborhood. It was the closest thing to a skyscraper amidst small boutiques and brownstones. She had the address that Jack and Holly had given her when they'd tracked her down that first week after she'd impulsively hopped on the plane to the States. Her friends had found her with alarming ease and had made her promise that she would go to Daniel if she needed any help.

Daniel was one of her grandfather's business partners—but he was also a friend, she reminded herself. She was certain he knew she was in the city but he and his wife, Ivy, had given her the space she'd asked for. They'd given her room to create a new life, one that had nothing to do with her grandfather's money or expectations.

And she'd done a hell of a job. Six weeks into her "new life" and she was about to beg a family friend for money so she could run back home. Lucia paused before the glass doors of the hotel and drew in a long deep breath of the cool fall air. Maybe she should ask Jack and Holly if she could stay with them in Paris instead. But that would just be delaying the inevitable. She let out an exhale with a loud sigh and pulled open the heavy door.

The hotel smelled cozy and clean—like a home away from home. Which it was, she supposed, for the wealthy and famous who could afford to stay at a place like this. The lobby was quiet but the clerk behind the front desk was busy talking to guests who appeared to be checking in.

Lucia paced around the reception area. She could wait; it wasn't like she was in a rush to humiliate herself. The lobby opened into a bar area, where an empty hostess stand stood and beyond that an empty restaurant sat perfectly set up, waiting for the next crowd.

Perching on a barstool, Lucia kept an eye on the front desk. Maybe she should have called first.

"Would you like to see a bar menu?"

Lucia swiveled around to find the bartender watching her expectantly.

"We're not serving dinner yet but we have some appetizers available."

The bartender was hot. Like, movie star hot. Lucia's mouth went dry and her ability to speak English took a momentary hiatus from her brain. This guy was intimidatingly hot. Dark hair and bright blue eyes with a chiseled jaw—he should play a superhero in a movie.

When one corner of his mouth turned up in an amused smile, Lucia came back to her senses. "No, thank you. I'm not hungry." Her stomach gave a little whine of protest but she ignored it. That nine dollars had to last her until she got home.

The bartender put away the little menu but didn't move. "Something to drink?"

Lucia shook her head. "No, thanks. I'm just here to meet someone."

The hot bartender's eyebrows lifted in new understanding. "Oh, you're here for the job?"

"Um...."

He looked down at his watch and then back to her with that amused, sexy-as-hell little smile. "You're early."

"Oh. Well, I...." Before she could finish, he tossed the dishrag he'd been holding under the bar and headed toward the register. "But you're in luck. I'm the one conducting the interviews so we can get started whenever you're ready."

Lucia watched him dig through a stack of papers next to the register. *Interviews?*

He came back to her and set a paper and pen in front of her. "Application for Employment" was printed across the top. Lucia felt a hysterical laugh building in her lungs, threatening to escape. A job? He thought she was here for a job?

Lucia picked up the pen and toyed with it as she scanned the questions. What was she even supposed to be applying for?

"Do you have any waitressing experience?" hot guy asked.

Ah. Well, that answered that. For a moment she considered lying but then thought better of it. "Not really." She glanced up to see the bartender's reaction but he was busy wiping down the glassware.

Lucia glanced over at the front desk to see if the clerk was available. She wondered if Daniel was even in the building. She had an image of him walking into the bar that he owned and finding his billionaire business partner's daughter bussing tables.

The laughter that had been threatening came out as a choking noise which caught the bartender's attention. "You all right?"

Lucia nodded as the bartender filled a glass of water and set it down in front of her. At that moment her stomach growled so loudly it would have been comical if it wasn't so mortifying.

"You sure you don't want to see that bar menu?"

Those piercing, sapphire eyes were filled with amusement as he rested his elbows on the bar, bringing his face closer to hers.

She shook her head. "No, thanks. I can't, uh....I mean, I don't have any money on me." The amusement faded and was replaced by a look of understanding that was so sweet and so welcome, it was enough to bring tears to her eyes.

"Well you're in luck because employees eat for free."

Lucia looked down at her still-blank application and then back up to the bartender. "I got the job?"

He laughed as he turned back to the register and started tapping at the screen. "Let's not get ahead of ourselves. But while you're interviewing, I think we can say you're practically staff."

He glanced at her over his shoulder. "I won't tell the big bosses if you don't."

Lucia thought of Daniel, the biggest of the big bosses at this hotel. "Your secret is safe with me."

That earned her a full-blown smile and—oh my God, the man had dimples. Full-on dimples, along with a cleft in his chin—it was the kind of smile one found on the underwear models gracing the billboards in Times Square, not your neighborhood bartender.

And that smile was focused on her. It was too much—like staring directly into the sun. Lucia dropped her head and pretended to study the blank application in front of her. The only sound around them was a busboy cleaning silverware at the far end of the bar and the distant sound of the front desk clerk dealing with the same guests who'd been hogging his attention since Lucia had arrived.

She heard the bartender moving toward her and started filling in the easy blanks. Her first name, her age....the last name she left blank. *What was she doing?* Her grandfather would have a fit if he found out she was applying to be a waitress.

But Grandpa isn't here.

That thought brought with it a now-familiar heady feeling of freedom. It was that terrifyingly exciting sense of leaping into the unknown that had gotten her through the past six weeks on her own in a foreign country. She'd paved her own way quite successfully for a little while there. Her friends in the fashion industry had set her up with an internship with Eleanor Fallone, one of the biggest up-and-comers in the business. Lucia had thrived in the fast-paced lifestyle and some fashion bloggers and buyers had even started to take an interest in some of her designs.

But then Eleanor had announced that she and her team were heading to London for the next show and there was no room on the team for an intern who couldn't pay her own way.

And while the internship had been an incredible learning experience, it was definitely not lucrative. She'd blown through the little savings she'd tucked away so until she could gain access to her trust fund...well, she was at her grandfather's mercy. A fact she just knew he was counting on. The trust her mother had set up before she died stipulated that she didn't get access to the money until she turned thirty...or until she married. *Please.* As if a ring on the finger meant instant financial responsibility. Or maybe her mother had fallen victim to the chauvinistic idea that men were better with money. She didn't remember her mother but that didn't sound like her. She was willing to bet her entire trust fund that the marriage exception had been inserted by her old-fashioned grandfather. Not that he was that chauvinistic—he was just that romantic. He'd had the perfect marriage and the perfect family and it was completely beyond him that not everyone lived and died for love.

"Hey, are you all right?"

Lucia's head shot up and she found the bartender watching her, the brilliant smile replaced by a frown of concern. Lucia glanced down to see that she was gripping the pen like a sword and she was dangerously close to tears for the fifth time that day. Drawing a deep breath, she forced a smile.

"I'm fine," she said. She loosened her death grip on the pen and gestured toward the application. "Just not sure this is the best idea...."

He leaned back against an ice bin and crossed his arms. "Do you need a job?"

Lucia fingered the nine dollars and thirty-six cents through her jeans pocket. "Desperately."

The corner of his lips twitched in amusement at her pathetic sigh. "So what's the problem?"

Lucia stared at him, her mouth open and ready to speak but no words came out. Was she actually considering doing this? Could she really get a job like any normal person her age? She could make her own money and stay in New York. Maybe she could even apply to the Fashion Institute like Eleanor had suggested.

Heart racing with excitement, Lucia's eye was caught by the blank spaces that she couldn't fill in. "I, uh...I don't have any experience."

The sympathetic look in his eyes was so sweet she thought she might melt. "Are you willing to learn?"

Lucia nodded with a little too much enthusiasm. "Absolutely."

He rewarded her with another swoon-worthy smile. "That's all I need to hear."

Lucia's eyebrows shot up in surprise. "So....I'm hired?" Her voice sounded squeaky to her own ears but she couldn't help it. The idea that anyone would hire her on the spot with no experience or references, well...it seemed like a miracle. Especially when she'd been moments away from calling it quits.

The universe works in mysterious ways, her grandfather would say.

The hot bartender leaned over the bar and clasped his hands. "Let's not get carried away," he said with a laugh. "You're hired on a probationary basis. We're understaffed so I'm allowed to hire a few new people. I'll start you out with some slow shifts and if it works out, you can pick up a normal workload. Deal?"

Lucia nodded. "Deal."

He went to take her application from her but paused when he saw all the blank spaces. "You're going to have to fill in the bare minimum here so we can put you on the payroll."

He pushed the paper back toward her along with the pen but Lucia paused before picking them up. The bartender seemed to notice because he leaned over further and spoke quietly. "Don't worry, the managers here don't dig too deep."

Her head shot up in surprise. Did he know who she was? Her grandfather had always shielded his children and grandchildren from the press but maybe he recognized her from the crazy publicity that surrounded Daniel and Ivy's wedding at the Brunelli estate. It had been impossible to avoid the media frenzy that had descended upon their little town in Tuscany and the Brunelli clan had found itself under a magnifying glass.

"I, uh, I can explain," she started.

The bartender shook his head. "No need. Believe me, you aren't the first person to come in here without working papers and you won't be the last."

Lucia blinked up at him. *Working papers?* And then it clicked into place. He thought she was worried about filling in her last name because she was in the country illegally. She almost laughed out loud in relief. While she had been raised in Italy, her mother had actually given birth to her in New York at a hospital in the Bronx so Lucia was fortunate enough to have dual citizenship. But there was no need to tell this kind stranger that. So instead she let him see her smile of genuine relief.

"Thank you."

For one brief moment their eyes met and she was sure he knew that she was keeping a secret. And in that split second, she had the overwhelming compulsion to tell this man everything. But then he smiled and the moment was over as he slid the paper out in his direction and snatched the pen out of her hands. "So, let's see here…" he drawled as he perused the blanks spaces.

Lucia let out a little laugh when he bent over the paper and started filling in the top section. "What are you doing?"

He ignored her as he scribbled something on another line.

"There," he said with finality as he slid it back toward her. "You're all set, Lucia."

A laugh bubbled up in her throat as she read his answers. "Lucia… Jones?" She arched a brow in disbelief. "Is that the best you could come up with?"

He shrugged. "What can I say, I'm not terribly creative with my lies. I've always heard that when it comes to lying, the simpler the better."

Lucia's eyes narrowed with mock suspicion. "And do you lie often?"

He plucked a straw from its holder and tossed it at her. "Only for damsels in distress."

That had her outright laughing. "Is that what I am? Here I thought I was the answer to your prayers." As soon as the words were out of her mouth she realized how flirtatious they sounded. Heat crept into her cheeks. "Because you're looking for a waitress, I mean."

His eyes were filled with teasing laughter and she waited for a mocking retort. But instead he let her off easy. "Of course."

Lucia shifted in her seat. This man was her new boss, she shouldn't be flirting. But he was so close and his eyes seemed so kind. It had been a while since anyone had flirted with her. She had been surrounded by women and gay men at the internship, with no time to meet people during her precious off hours. And here was this man, this kind, sexy, gorgeous…*nameless* man.

Lucia stuck out her hand. "Let's try this again. Hi, I'm Lucia *Jones*."

He laughed but took her hand in his. "Nice to meet you, Lucia Jones. I'm Ryan Smith."

www.ingramcontent.com/pod-product-compliance
Lightning Source LLC
Chambersburg PA
CBHW050755250626
47155CB00005B/2073